THE MONKEY KING
& OTHER STORIES

THE MONKEY KING

& OTHER STORIES

EDITED BY

GRIFFIN ONDAATJE

ILLUSTRATIONS BY

DAVID BOLDUC

HarperPerennial
HarperCollins*Publishers*Ltd

"Foreword," © 1995 Graeme MacQueen; "Introduction," © 1995 Griffin Ondaatje; "The Monkey King," © 1995 Shyam Selvadurai; "How the Landlord Went to Heaven," © 1974 George Keyt; "Brighter Still," © 1995 Graeme MacQueen; "Lord Krishna and Kaliya" © 1995 Mira Mishra; "The Chola King," © 1995 Tim Wynne-Jones; "The Resting Hill," © 1995 Griffin Ondaatje; "The Deer, the Tortoise and the Kaerala Bird," © 1995 J. B. Disanayaka; "Water Under a Rock," © 1995 George Woodcock; "Two Friends by the Villu," © 1995 Ranjini Obeyesekere; "The Vulture," © 1995 Michael Ondaatje; "The Hopper," © 1995 Raj Ramanathapillai; "The Dog Who Drank from Socks," © 1995 Griffin Ondaatje; "Narada's Lesson," © 1995 P.K. Page; "Power Misused," © 1995 S. Samarasinghe; "The Unicorn and the Grapevine," © 1995 Pebble Productions Inc.; "Kundalini," © 1995 Chitra Fernando; "Scarless Face," © 1995 Griffin Ondaatje; "The Cycle of Revenge," © 1995 M. G. Vassanji; "The Monkey and the Crocodile," © 1995 Raj Ramanathapillai; "Garuda and the Snake," © 1995 Griffin Ondaatje; "Just Like the Rest," © 1995 Graeme MacQueen; "The Rupee," © 1995 S.M. Lena; "Is the River Asleep?" © 1995 Sarah Sheard; "Hanuman and Sita," © 1995 Rajiva Wijesinha; "Angulimala," © 1995 Michael Ondaatje; "Two Stories of Andare the Court Jester," © 1974 George Keyt; "The Road to Butterfly Mountain," © 1979 Manel Ratnatunga; "A Changed Snake," © 1995 David Bolduc; "Akbar and Birbal," © 1995 Graeme MacQueen; "Mouthful of Pearls," © 1995 Judith Thompson; "The Camel Who Cried in the Sun," © 1995 Griffin Ondaatje; "How the Gods and Demons Learned to Play Together," © 1995 Ernest MacIntyre; "The Great Journey," © 1995 Linda Spalding; "Fate and Fortune," © 1995 Graeme MacQueen; "Tell It to the Walls," © 1995 Diane Schoemperlen.

Illustrations copyright © 1995 by David Bolduc. Except illustration by Richard Henriquez which appears on page 75. Used by permission.

First Edition: 1995

Canadian Cataloguing in Publication Data

Main entry under title:
The monkey king & other stories

ISBN 0-00-647940-5

1. Tales — Sri Lanka.   2. Canadian fiction (English) — 20th century.*
3. Short stories, Canadian (English).* I. Ondaatje, Griffin.

PS8329.M65 1995   398.2'095493   C95-930440-1
PR9197.32.M65 1995

---

95 96 97 98 99 ❖ HC 10 9 8 7 6 5 4 3 2 1

Printed and bound in the United States

For Mom and Dad

CONTENTS

FOREWORD

The tale is just like this little sapling. It develops, you prune it, graft it, clean it, and it sprouts branches, leaves, and fruit. A life develops . . .

Hungarian storyteller quoted by Linda Degh,
Folktales and Society

The stories in this book have been dear to people in Sri Lanka for many years. Some of them began on the island and some began elsewhere and were welcomed, adopted, retold by Sri Lankans. In this book you will find them retold yet again, this time mainly by Canadian writers. This is both a respectful borrowing from Sri Lanka and a tribute to all the people, wherever they have lived, who have passed on these tales.

Stories, by their very nature, resist being captured and owned by any one culture, race, nation. Some stories are especially fond of travelling, and these are the ones chosen for this volume. They speak to our common needs as human beings: our loneliness, our fear, our love and our ability to find the universe funny. They remind us that we belong on the earth, and make us laugh at our efforts to get to heaven by holding on to the tail of the divine elephant ("How the Landlord Went to Heaven"); but they also push us beyond ourselves. They won't leave us alone. The Prophet won't let us forget about the camel we left sweltering in the sun; Vishnu subverts our picture of everyday reality; the Monkey King won't let us be comfortable in our suspicion and cynicism.

These tales don't suffer from culture shock when they are brought to Canada because they have already been on the road a long time.

Many of the stories of the Prophet have travelled across half of Asia before finding their way to Sri Lanka. Hindu stories have been going back and forth between Sri Lanka and India for centuries. Buddhist tales have been welcomed in many different countries.

The story of Angulimala is a fine example of a travelling tale. This Buddhist story began, as far as we can trace its beginning, in North India several centuries before the Christian era. It found its way in the Pali language, after who knows how many tellings, to Sri Lanka, where it was valued and kept alive. This is the version that our retelling is based on. But the story remained popular in India for a long while. The Chinese Buddhist monk Hsuan-tsang, who undertook a perilous journey to India beginning in A.D. 629, describes in his account of his travels the great monument built just outside the ruined city of Savatthi in north-east India to honour Angulimala's conversion by the Buddha. Hsuan-tsang eagerly retells the story of Angulimala for his Chinese readers, but as a matter of fact the tale had by his time already reached China. In fact, there exist today at least nine distinct Chinese versions of it, ranging from brief tales similar to the Pali one, through several cheerfully expanded versions, to a full-blown Mahayana sutra—a literary production of great sophistication. The story finds life today throughout Asia in unexpected forms. A friend tells me of having recently seen a theatrical production of it in Sri Lanka by a troupe of gay men. In Thailand, women seeking a safe childbirth give offerings to the image of Angulimala. Now, with this book, we have yet another version, yet more life breathed into Angulimala. As the storyteller says, "you prune it, graft it, clean it . . . A life develops."

The retelling of a story is necessary because of change and human difference. Different times, different cultures. But retelling is possible only because of the human nature we share. We are all able to follow a narrative. And when we retell these stories we become part of a community stretching back in time and reaching forward into the future. We participate in the magic spoken of in "The Unicorn and the Grapevine": we talk to those not yet born, we hear the dead speak to us as clearly and urgently as the person in the next room.

Moreover, while stories are one of the strongest testimonies to our common human nature, they also testify to the restlessness of this nature. We don't stay the same. Our nature is not finished. We try to remake ourselves, and stories are part of the effort. We become more compassionate and just as we weave these tales, as we transmit them and as we live them.

You may wonder why we are transmitting tales of friendship, reconciliation and non-violence from Sri Lanka at a time when the island is still reeling from the appalling violence and war of the past years. I will leave it to the editor to tell the story of how the book came about, but I should say that my own involvement was directly related to the political situation in Sri Lanka. It was at a conference called Linking Human Rights and Development in Sri Lanka, sponsored by South Asia Partnership, that I first met Griffin Ondaatje. I was at the conference representing the Centre for Peace Studies at McMaster University as well as a project funded by the Partners for Children Fund called "The Health of Children in War Zones." I wasn't thinking about stories at all when I met Griffin; I was thinking about what Canadians could contribute to the building of peace and justice in Sri Lanka. I received a pleasant jolt when he told me of his proposal for the book. I was encouraged to stop thinking for a moment about what we could give to Sri Lanka and to think about what we might learn from Sri Lanka.

But perhaps Sri Lankans will take some interest in our retellings. Even before the guns stop firing, a society that has been at war begins the process of healing. This healing is a complex process and it faces many obstacles, but it may succeed if enough wit, tenacity and compassion are brought together. Stories have their part to play in this healing. I see this volume as a little offering to the people of Sri Lanka, given with the deepest gratitude, at a time when both yearning and hope are high.

Graeme MacQueen
January 1, 1995

ACKNOWLEDGEMENTS

I'm very grateful to have had the chance to work on this book, and would like to thank the staff and board of directors of World Literacy of Canada for giving me the opportunity.

Work on the project covered a period of about a year and a half. I would like to thank Mamta Mishra for her inspiration and thoughtfulness, and for helping from the beginning to achieve the book's overall design and aim.

I'm very thankful also to Graeme MacQueen for his kind encouragement and generosity, and for his constant editorial contributions throughout the development of the book.

Thanks to Chitra Ranawake and the Sri Lanka Canada Development Fund for their help and support. I'm very appreciative also of the help of Stephanie Garrow, Kate Blackstone, Sarath Chandrasekere, Raj Ramanathapillai and Rick McCutcheon. Thanks to Ida Hersi, Barbara Mencke and Peter Folkins.

I'd like to give special thanks to my editor at HarperCollins, Maya Mavjee; to all the Sri Lankan and Canadian authors who contributed retellings; and to David Bolduc for creating great original illustrations for the book.

INTRODUCTION

When I first started working on this book I knew very little about Eastern legends and folklore. What I knew of Sri Lanka I had learned through personal visits to the island, staying with cousins and relatives and travelling to towns and parts of the countryside. The first time I went to Sri Lanka I was twelve and it was a shock to me getting off the plane in Colombo. Checking a journal I kept then, I see from the first page that I'd thought I was going to India: *Sunday, 20, 2, 78. We go to India today . . . the air cab driver started telling us about when he just about jumped into a bunch of sharks . . . .* But at that age it wouldn't have mattered where I was going. The real shock was entering a new country, and waking up in the morning on the first day, walking through a house where all the doors were open and sensing that, outside, there were new colours, smells, the heat of a place I didn't know anything about. At that age my image of any country outside of Canada was based on movies. While staying on the island for four months I lost a lot of that perception. Following aunts and uncles who'd guide us through the new setting we were in, I had the freedom to fall into it all, and daydream, without thinking how far we were from home. And it wasn't until we got back to Canada, where the car tires made no sound on the highway, that I felt that things had changed somehow. I was glad to be back in Canada, but I was sad too because I missed my cousins and the ocean and the food, and the trip remained a very visual block of time in my memory.

I've learned a bit more about Sri Lanka since then, and about some of its history and the traditions of Buddhism and Hinduism, though from the start it was my general interest in folktales, and Buddhist and

Hindu legends, that helped me shape the concept for this book. Over the past year, through reading and research and with the help and encouragement from Canadian and Sri Lankan friends, I've gained a broader understanding of the traditions of storytelling. It has been an interesting book of stories to put together. It seemed that whoever I talked to had some link to tales through childhood, and many people brought an enthusiasm and open-eyed spirit to the whole project when they were asked if they would contribute with a tale or a retelling.

Some of the most important editorial help I received came from Professor Graeme MacQueen—a Religious Studies teacher and Pali scholar at McMaster University. Graeme took time to translate and retell several of the Pali tales and *Jataka* legends we used in the book. Through research of previously published material in English, and through the help of other contacts in Canada and Sri Lanka, I was able to gather many stories from Sinhalese and Tamil sources. I've made no attempt to represent all the religions of Sri Lanka, and so there aren't retellings of Christian-based stories, though I did receive and collect a number of Muslim tales. Also it became clear early on that it wouldn't be a book of oral folktales or legends entirely indigenous to Sri Lanka. Stories cross borders continually, and many of these stories have origins in India. It seemed best to accept a wide variety of stories, to collect a mixture of religious legends, myths, local folklore and popular children's stories from Sri Lanka. I decided that the tales selected should be ones well known in Sri Lanka over generations. The majority of the tales and legends we looked at were told on the island centuries ago and are still well known and retold in homes, classrooms and temples.

The decision to collect and organize the tales as retellings allowed me to get longer versions of some tales that, in their original version, recollection or translation, were too brief or too formal for the kind of book I wanted to put together. Retellings loosened things up and allowed me to involve Canadian and Sri Lankan writers who could bring new voices to the tales. To the Canadian authors I wrote to, the request probably came out of the blue since they'd never seen these tales before, and seeing what they chose to do in a retelling was encouraging. It was like getting help in smuggling goods over a border. Some retellings followed the lead of an original tale closely, while others made wide departures. Several of the authors decided to lift the story-line up through the surface of time, so that the characters appear fresh in present-day settings. Each writer was asked to keep the main themes and story-lines roughly the same, which they have, and so these retellings still carry their original messages.

Through all of these changes most of the retellings still fall into the landscape of folktales—a deer gently persuades a king to stop harming other creatures; a snake flees to a hermit for protection; a man refuses to go to heaven unless his dog can go too. About a third of the retellings in *The Monkey King & Other Stories* find their source in Buddhist legends, the group of tales known as the *Jataka* tales. The *Jataka* is a collection of about 550 stories of the Buddha's previous lives or incarnations. They are stories that are well known in South Asia and especially popular in Sri Lanka. They were brought to the island and translated into Sinhalese about two thousand years ago. The Buddha was said to have told these tales as instructional stories to illuminate certain principles to monks and nuns. As he recalls episodes from his previous lives, the Buddha tells of being many creatures—dogs, deer, vultures, tree-spirits, merchants.

Among the other stories in the book are several legends of Hindu gods. Two retellings are based on stories from the ancient Hindu epics the *Ramayana* and the *Mahabharata*. Folkstories or secular tales, from either Sinhalese or Tamil sources, form most of the remainder of the book. Yet in total there are only thirty-five stories retold here, and so the life of the oral storytelling tradition in Sri Lanka is reflected in only a small way. Though I feel this book transmits some aspects of the religions and cultures in Sri Lanka, there are many more kinds of forums for *tellings* of legends, folktales and parables that can't be conveyed in a book. A strong bond of storytelling commonly exists between grandparents and grandchildren, for example, and among the small crowds gathered at night around a village storyteller. Tales also get retold on pilgrimage routes. It's common to see groups of pilgrims gathered together near sacred sites, resting and telling stories. These spontaneous forums allow for a kind of mid-journey reflection, which is what stories give us in our lives. Sharing stories becomes an essential aspect of the pilgrimage. I received a letter from a Buddhist monk who travels most of the year, walking to villages throughout central Sri Lanka, telling oral folktales to anyone who will listen. This is something hard to imagine happening in a city or a suburb in Canada.

Festivals at sacred sites in Sri Lanka can have a unifying effect on people, often bringing together Buddhists, Hindus, Muslims and Christians on the same pilgrimage routes. Pilgrims who walk up the mountain known as Sri Pada (to Buddhists), Sivanolipadam (to Hindus) and Adam's Peak (to Muslims and Christians) climb the steps together through the night and share the view at dawn. In Kataragama, a city in the south-east of the island where Hindu gods such as Ganesh and Skanda are important for both Hindus and Buddhists, there seems to be an interconnectedness that rises above concerns or differences of religious background. Hinduism and Buddhism especially are very closely related—the origins of Buddhist philosophy having grown out of Hinduism. In Anuradhapura, in the north central province, where the giant bo-tree has stood for over two thousand years since being replanted from India as a sapling of the original Bodhi tree (the tree under which the Buddha attained enlightenment), many Buddhists gather and pray beneath its branches. And still, outside religious festivals or sermons, Sri Lankan children can easily absorb the many stories and legends told through art. Sculpture is everywhere, and folk-drama and songs are further forums in which legends and tales are told. Children may even read comic-book versions of the blue god Krishna, or of Siva, Hanuman and Ganesh—or of the hundreds of *Jataka* tales.

Tales are transplanted and grow in new places, just as the banyan sapling took root in Anuradhapura. Branches of stories grow in all directions. In one book of translations, an editor mentions that "Chaucer unwittingly puts a *Jataka* story into the mouth of his Pardoner . . . ." Finding out who told a tale first, or where it travelled from can be like looking at one star, letting the rest of the sky black out slowly. You look away, or someone bumps the telescope, and you look back and see a thousand more stars.

People will always look at stars and read tales, wherever they come from. Rereading the tales in *The Monkey King & Other Stories* I see it as a book for adults as well as kids. Some retellings, such as "Andare," appear to be for children, while others, such as "Mouthful of Pearls," reach an older audience.

We try to gather in the world and its stories at any age. William Blake writes in a poem that an ear is like "a whirlpool fierce to draw creations in." As kids we drew creations in with a special sense of urgency. It seemed in those day we were a bit like dogs, used to the outskirts of language, crossing fences that people put up years ago. We took in stories that most adults would automatically glance beyond and walk past since these stories were myths or there were animals in them that talked. Yet animals were there to bring us some of the wild and the silence that roamed further off stage. And in this way folktales and legends seemed to get things right somehow, because there was so much new wilderness around us at the time. Even at formal gatherings, with our bad table manners, it was as if we felt more at ease in the wild—like those animals at the end of fables who, invited to the King's garden party, still chose to sit at tables close to the fields. Dreams from across night time, characters from a book, television channels, moods—everything got picked up and flowed easily through our minds. We took our time, pausing in the middle of a busy sidewalk to examine an ant. And so we'd begin to sense the individuality and ancientness of things, and the mystery behind it all too. Kids don't have the same sense of time or boundaries as adults have. And I don't think stories have this sense of boundary either.

Still, by the time we become adults many of us have put a lot of distance between ourselves and folktales or legends—we went over that ground back in childhood, got out of that forest long ago. The stories are left on the horizon, and become a kind of landmark to an old way of seeing things. We become less ancient ourselves, in a way, and more familiar with present worlds.

In the journal I kept for my first ten days in Sri Lanka, it's strange to find practically no descriptions of landmarks or new scenery. I remember the places we went to on the island, but most of the things I mentioned in my journal are meals, card games, the ocean, and *stories*. We went swimming on our second day in Sri Lanka: *Wednesday, 24,2,78 . . . we body surfed and everything. The waves reminded me of a movie called "Ride the Wild Surf" on channel 11, the Saturday morning movie. It was one of those movies when the hero surfs, gets hurt and loses his girlfriend, then he wins one of those surfing contests and then she says "Oh Frank I always knew you were for me . . . ."*

We move in our own world as kids, and bring it with us wherever we go. Maybe we still do that as adults—carry other stories beside our own. Folktales and legends hold still for us, let us catch up, and they reveal new meanings when we let them travel alongside us. This book carries tales and legends from the East, which may travel alongside you and keep retelling stories beside your own.

Griffin Ondaatje

THE MONKEY KING

RETOLD BY SHYAM SELVADURAI

A YOUNG NOBLEMAN ONCE found himself in charge of a rebel-held island that had been recaptured by the King's forces. The island was very small and had only one town in it. The nobleman's name was Jeevan, which meant life, and he loved life. He was a tall man with fine black hair that glinted in the sun and one of his pleasures was, when he patrolled the town, to ride in his open jeep, standing up, the wind playing in his hair. It gave the inhabitants of the town much gladness to see him ride by, for they felt that someone who got such pleasure from the wind in his hair must surely value life, whether his or theirs. Here, they felt, was a protector. Someone who would prevent the King's forces from wreaking the havoc they had caused in so many other recaptured domains. There was also another reason that the inhabitants loved watching him: among them, there was not a single young man, all their youth having joined the rebel forces or been killed by the King's army.

The nobleman was from the capital city and had never been to such a small, rustic island before. He found the simplicity and meagreness of the dwellings charming rather than distasteful, the lack of luxuries such as electricity and piped water quaint rather than a burden. He also loved the townspeople and found them quite different from what he had imagined. He had been taught that these people, the enemy, were cruel and dangerous. Instead he found them friendly and courteous, and liked their unhurried way of walking and the way they would sit around in circles at night, spinning yarns. He kept the gates of his bungalow open and every evening some of them would gather on his verandah and engage in a contest of storytelling.

The young nobleman had discovered a novelty. Coming from the capital city, he had never bathed at a well before and this became something he looked forward to every evening, the sensation of the cold water on his skin washing away the tiredness of the day. How much more refreshing the buckets of water were, he thought, compared to the tepid showers in the capital city.

His well baths were observed by the women of the town who passed by on their way to collect firewood to cook the evening meal. Even though he was a representative of a King they hated, a King who had brought great devastation to their lives, they found themselves stirred by the sight of this young man, clad only in a wet half sarong.

Unknown to the nobleman, he was also observed by the venerable old Monkey King who sat in a kumbuk tree not far from the well. The monkey, who was really the Bodhisatthva in one of his reincarnations, seemed to draw no pleasure from the sight of the bathing man. Rather, so the monkeys in his retinue observed, he wore a troubled frown as he watched the young man draw water from the well. When asked by his followers why he was uneasy, he shook his head as if he too did not know the cause of it. The monkeys thought it was only the nobleman that disturbed their master, but there was another reason for the troubled frown on the Monkey King's face. For, in his troupe was Devadatta, the worst enemy of the Bodhisatta, disguised as a monkey. Even as the Monkey King knew this, he also knew that he could not reveal this knowledge to his subjects. It was the workings of fate and even he, the Bodhisatta, had to submit to it.

One day, from the convoy of women who passed by the well, a young boy detached himself and came to stand a little distance from the nobleman. He was a beautiful, healthy looking boy. Yet the sight of him brought no pleasure to the Monkey King. The nobleman, who had just drawn some water, rested his bucket on the rim of the well and looked at the boy. The boy smiled and his smile was shy and friendly. "Hello, malli," the nobleman called out, addressing the boy as young brother to show that he should not be afraid to approach if he wished. Yet the boy remained where he was, his hands behind his back.

The next day, the boy detached himself from the group of women again, and this time he drew a little closer. Once again, the nobleman called to the boy, but he remained where he was, smiling shyly but never answering the nobleman's questions.

Gradually, over the week, the boy drew closer and closer until one day he was standing right by the well. The nobleman had grown used to the attention of the silent boy and, after greeting him, he turned away to draw a bucket of water. In that instant, the Monkey King saw, behind the boy's back, a glint of metal. So great was his shock that he lost his balance and had to cling to a branch to prevent himself from falling to the ground. The rustling of the branch drew the attention of the nobleman and he turned just in time to see the boy draw the dagger from behind his back and prepare to plunge it into him. Crying out, he grasped the boy's wrist and, with a quick movement, twisted the boy's hand behind his back. The dagger fell to the ground as he brought the boy to his knees.

"Who made you do this?" the nobleman cried.

Now, for the first time, the boy spoke, but his words were shocking in the hatred and venom they spat out at the nobleman and his King. There must have been some charm, some power in the words of the boy, for, as he shouted out his words of loathing, a madness seemed to seize hold of the nobleman and he grabbed the dagger from the ground and plunged it into the boy. The boy cried out triumphantly, as if he had achieved what he wanted, and fell dead at the nobleman's feet.

The nobleman backed away from the boy, accidentally knocking the bucket off the rim of the well. The water ran around the boy and mixed with his blood, carrying it away in little rivulets along the ground. The nobleman drew himself together. He collected his towel and soap and began to walk away from the well towards the town. As he walked, he looked around him and it was as if his eyes were opened for the first time. For he now saw that the simple dwellings, to which he had attributed such charm, were actually modest due to the exigency of war rather than choice, that the lack of luxuries was not quaint but debilitating. As he looked at the people he passed, he saw, for the first time, the numb suffering in their eyes even as they smiled at him, the distended bellies of the malnourished children. How many of them had known of the boy and his evil intent he wondered, how many had actually collaborated in putting that dagger in that child's hand.

That evening the story of what had happened spread through the town and among the King's forces. The nobleman waited for a delegation to come from the town to express their concern about the event, but none came.

While he was at dinner that evening the captain of the forces asked permission to speak with him and was granted entry.

"Sir," he said, once he had saluted the nobleman smartly, "there is much anger among the troops on your behalf, but also fear. Unless there is some reprisal, our lives, and especially your life, will not be safe." The nobleman continued to eat his meal and after a few moments the captain wondered if he had not been understood or heard. Then he realized the significance of his leader's silence.

That night the Monkey King and his retinue were woken by a scream. It came from some part of the town. The cry was now picked up and echoed in other parts and soon the entire town seemed to be calling out in pain and grief.

The Monkey King gathered his followers around him.

"Friends," he said, "the happenings in the town promise no good for us. Surely man's enmity, once they have turned against one another, will be unleashed on us too. Let us, therefore, go up the river to a safer place."

So that night they travelled up the river to a grove of trees that was far away from the town. The grove was populated with large mango trees that had the most succulent, the most delicious fruits in the whole country. The flesh of these mangoes was firm not stringy and, when one bit into it, the juice did not flow in runny driblets but seeped out, the consistency of honey.

Much as the monkeys would have liked to share this discovery with the townspeople, they feared for their lives because of what had taken place in the town. In order to guard their secret, the Monkey King instructed his subjects to pluck and eat the flowers of the mango trees whose branches leaned over the river. What the Monkey King dreaded was that a mango might fall off a tree, be washed downriver and discovered by the townspeople or the King's forces. Then they would certainly come looking for the trees, plunder the mangoes and even kill and drive out the monkeys.

Devadatta, the Bodhisatta's enemy, was assigned a specific branch that stretched far over the river. On this branch was an ants' nest and, hidden behind it, Devadatta one day found a small, green mango.

Because of its location, it had escaped his attention before. Instead of plucking and eating it, Devadatta draped some leaves over the mango, so that none of the other monkeys would discover it.

In the month that passed many things changed. The nobleman gave up his greatest pleasure of riding with the wind in his hair because it was too dangerous. In fact, he hardly left the compound of his bungalow for fear of his life and he assigned the task of patrolling the town to the King's forces. His gates were now closed to the townspeople, and their petitions he only heard through the captain of the army. Often the townspeople, whose concerns had been ignored by the captain, would knock on his gate and call out to him to attend to their needs. But he merely shut his windows and let his dogs out into the compound. All the hatred and distrust he had been taught to feel towards these people now came back to him. On the rare occasion that he had to ride through the town, he kept his eyes averted from everything around him, so profound had his distaste become for the island and its people.

Meanwhile, the mango grew into a round, succulent fruit. When it reached maturity, it became too heavy for its stem, broke off and floated down the river.

That evening, the nobleman came down to the river to bathe for he no longer used the well. He had brought with him guards from the King's army. Even though the river at this time of day was beautiful, the rays of the setting sun sparkling on the ripples of water, it brought him no pleasure.

He had finished his bath and was drying himself on the bank when he saw the mango floating down the river towards him. He commanded one of his soldiers to wade into the water and bring it to him. When the nobleman smelled the mango, he could tell it was a fine fruit. He borrowed a knife from a guard, cut the fleshy sides of the mango and ate them, marvelling at the extraordinary sweetness of the fruit.

All through dinner, the nobleman thought of that mango. It was the only thing that had brought him any enjoyment in the last month and it had made him aware of just how bereft his life had been of joy.

Finally he sent for the captain of the army and told him about the mango. "Surely, sir, it will not be hard to find the tree," the captain said. "It is clear that the branches hang over the river. All we have to do is follow the river upstream until we get to the tree."

So the next evening, the nobleman, the captain and a group of soldiers set off upstream in a boat. They had to travel quite a distance and it was almost nightfall before they found the grove. It was quiet and peaceful, for the Monkey King and his subjects having gone to dine at a group of plantain trees deeper in the jungle. The nobleman and his group plucked and ate as many mangoes as they wished. When they had finished, they rested under the trees for a few moments. As the nobleman sat on the grass, leaning against a tree trunk, he listened to the wind in the leaves above him and experienced a peace he had not felt in a long time. Here, he knew, he was safe from the dangers of the town. "Let us stay for the night," he said, turning to the captain.

The captain looked at him in surprise, but, not wanting to question the wishes of his leader, he directed the soldiers to build a fire under one of the trees. He prepared a bed for the nobleman from leaves and grass, which he covered with a blanket. That night, the nobleman lay on his bed, looking up at the stars until he finally fell asleep.

Just before dawn, the monkeys returned, bounding into the grove and springing from tree to tree, chattering away, unaware of the humans below them. The noise they made woke the nobleman and his companions. The nobleman sat up in his bed and searched around for his torch, for it was not quite day yet. He turned it on and shone it into the trees, catching the monkeys in its beam. His companions, who had now woken too, did the same and soon the trees above were illuminated. "A band of thieving monkeys have arrived to steal our mangoes," cried the nobleman. "Quick, get your guns and shoot them. Today we will have roasted monkey flesh with our mangoes!"

The monkeys now dashed to the tree on which their king sat and cried out "Sir, what are we to do? How are we to escape?"

The Monkey King looked down and then around him, "Do not fear," he said.

With that, he jumped from tree to tree until he arrived at the branch that had the ants' nest. He went along this branch to its edge and then, gathering himself together, he made a mighty leap, hurling himself through the air and across the river. Once on the opposite side, he contemplated the distance to the branch. Then he cut a long bamboo shoot at the root and stripped it until it was the consistency of a rope. His plan was to tie one end of the bamboo shoot to a tree on this side of the river and the other end to his waist. Then he would spring through the air to the other side and tie the shoot to the branch with the ants' nest, thus creating a cord along which his followers and he could swing to safety. He forgot, however, to calculate for the extra length of bamboo shoot that would be wrapped around his waist. So when he made his mighty leap again, hurling himself through the air, the shoot was not long enough. He was only able to grasp the end of the branch, without pulling himself onto it for safety. By now, the soldiers had surrounded the tree and were ready, with their guns pointed at the monkeys. The Monkey King, seeing this, signalled to his followers crying, "Go quickly, with good luck, treading on my back and across the bamboo shoot!" The monkeys were reluctant, but since their leader had commanded them, they did so, walking across the Monkey King's back and then swinging across the bamboo shoot to safety. The captain, below, raised his hand to give the command to shoot, but the nobleman, who had been watching the Monkey King's actions with interest, called out to the captain to hold his fire. "This is surely no ordinary monkey," he said. "I suspect he is some god in disguise."

The dawn was now breaking as the last of the monkeys began to cross the river. The Monkey King felt himself tiring, felt his hands ache with having to hold on to the branch, but so great was his love for his followers and so seriously did he take his responsibility as their leader that he held on, his head bent so they could step over it too if they needed. Finally, he did not feel any more monkeys on his back and, wondering if they had all crossed, he raised his head. One monkey remained and when he saw him, the Monkey King's blood froze in fear. It was Devadatta. Their eyes met for a moment and the Monkey

King saw the evil in Devadatta's face. Yet, he could not let go of the branch for some of his followers were still swinging across the shoot to the other side. In an instant, Devadatta sprang to the branch above. Then, letting out a shout of victory, he jumped, landing on the Monkey King's back and breaking his ribs. The Monkey King cried out as one of the ribs pierced his heart. A maddening pain coursed through his body but he still held on. Devadatta now swung quickly across the river to the other side.

The nobleman called one of his guards to climb the tree and bring the Monkey King down. Then, he had the Monkey King laid out on his bed. He knelt by him and said, "You made yourself a bridge for them to pass to safety. What are you to them and what are they to you?"

The Monkey King replied, "I am their king, their master and lord. When they were stricken with fear and grief they turned to me. By clinging to that branch, my subjects passed over to safety. I fear not death, for the happiness of those over whom I rule has been won." He turned to the nobleman. "You who are in many ways a king know this — not fear, but a straight sceptre is what gives a king his triumph. For a king who does not do justice each day will lose his land." Saying that, the Monkey King died.

The nobleman rose to his feet and, calling his guards, he instructed them to get the boat ready. Then he conveyed the Monkey King's body to the other side so that his subjects could perform all the necessary honours. This done, he bade his followers set a course downstream towards the town. The nobleman stood at the helm thinking about what the Monkey King had said. He looked around him and he was conscious, after a long time, of the beauty surrounding him. But the pleasure it brought him was now tempered by his awareness of the impermanence of everything. As the boat began to pick up speed, the nobleman felt the wind slowly begin to play against his face and hair.

HOW THE LANDLORD
WENT TO HEAVEN

RETOLD BY G. KEYT

A LANDLORD USED TO GO every morning to his paddy field to look after the tender rice plants that were growing there and to keep away straying cattle.

One day he was surprised to see a portion of the field in a bad state, with the rice plants either eaten up or damaged and uprooted. He saw large imprints in the mud as if a mortar had been taken about there and pressed down all over the place.

He was very angry and went among the village people asking, "Why do you allow your mortars to get into my field? Why not be more careful if your mortars are like that, and why not tie them up at night?"

The village people at first laughed at him as they thought he was joking, but knowing him to be a foolish man, they went to the field and saw the large round imprints. They said, "Sir, these are the footprints of an elephant. You had better keep watch tonight."

The landlord replied, "There are no elephants here. We have none, and there are no wild elephants in these parts. How can it be an elephant?" But the villagers said that it was an elephant that had come to his field and that he should keep watch for it in the night.

So that night the landlord went out and stood among the trees on a side of the field and kept a look out for the elephant. After a long time a glow like moonlight fell on his field and he looked up and saw a shining elephant the colour of silver coming down slowly from the sky. He could not believe his eyes.

As it came down and stood in his field, he ran to his house crying, "There is a chance of going to heaven. Come, all of you, come soon. We can go to heaven." His wife heard this and asked, "What is it you say? Go to heaven?"

"Yes," the landlord said, "come soon and call the others too!"

So she called the grandfather and the aunts and the daughter and the son-in-law and the children and they all ran off after the landlord.

He took them to the field and showed them the wonderful elephant, which was by this time walking about the field eating up the tender rice plants and trampling lots of them and making holes everywhere with its large feet. "This elephant came from heaven," he said.

"I saw it come down. Listen. I shall go and cling to its tail, and you, lady, cling to me, and one by one all the rest of you cling on after that. It will go back up to heaven."

He ran along the banks of the field and his wife and the others followed him and he clung to the tail of the elephant. His wife clung to him and one by one the rest clung on after that.

The elephant began to climb up into the sky with the landlord and the others all clinging on behind. As the elephant rose higher and higher and was going through the clouds, the landlord said to his wife: "It will be wonderful up there."

She asked, "Will there be nice paddy fields?"

"*Of course* there will be paddy fields, and much better than the paddy fields we have."

"Will they be bigger than the ones anywhere here, and do you think the rice plants are bigger too, and better than ours?" she asked.

"*Of course* it must be so," he answered.

Then she thought a while and asked, "What about the way they measure things? Are the measuring boxes much bigger than ours? And how big?"

The landlord said, "Oh well . . . as big or bigger than *this*," and he spread his hands out wide to show how big the measuring boxes were in heaven. He let go the tail of the elephant and suddenly fell and all those clinging to another fell. The whole lot fell and down they went and landed with a big splash in the mud of their paddy field.

BRIGHTER STILL

RETOLD BY GRAEME MACQUEEN

A LONG, LONG TIME AGO, when kings ruled in Benares and Kosala and everywhere else, and magical things happened more often than they do now, a king named Brahmadatta ruled in Benares. He was healthy and wealthy, but he was not wise. Like so many kings of Benares before him he was interested only in war and hunting, and since war was dangerous he preferred hunting. His favourite game were deer, and wherever the deer went he followed joyfully. He would fly pell-mell over freshly planted fields in his chariot, scattering arrows in all directions. Children, dogs and cows would take to their heels. He would recruit bearers and beaters to help with the hunt, and he would think nothing of taking away every able-bodied man from a village to scare up a stag for him, even at harvest time! When the peasants saw him coming they did not jump for joy and they did not hug each other with glee. They looked at the ground and shook their heads mournfully.

One day, the people of the villages gathered together and said to one another, "This king has become a serious bother. What can we do?" Someone said, "Why don't we build a big park with a high wall and a sturdy gate? Then we can round up all the deer in the district and put them inside it. When the King wants a deer he can go and get one without troubling us. It will be a lot of work, but it will be worth it." Everyone thought this was a splendid idea.

"But," said a woman who had just arrived from Kosala and did not know the region well, "where will we find the deer?"

"Easy," replied another woman. "We have two big herds with five hundred animals each. They live near a huge banyan tree by the river and their leaders are the most beautiful deer in the world. One is the colour of gold, so bright that it hurts your eyes when you look at him. We call him Brighter Than the Sun. The other, although it seems impossible, is even brighter, so that's what we call him: Brighter Still. Although these leaders are wise, there are many foolish deer in their herds, and perhaps we can use the foolish ones to trap the others."

Now, the leaders of the two herds had done good deeds in their previous lives, and this is why they were reborn with so many good qualities. Brighter Still was none other than the Great Being, who would one day become the Buddha.

So off went the peasants, and they fashioned a great park with brooks and ponds and thickets—just the sort of thing deer like. They made sure it had plenty of pasture. Then they tricked the more gullible deer with treats, flashing lights, penny whistles and puppet shows, so that soon they were streaming into the park as happy as larks, completely unaware that they were being trapped. Then more deer, reassured by the presence of the first group in the park, began to follow. The wise leaders found their warnings cast aside as the deer munched fresh grass, drank from the cool waters and carried out ceaseless propaganda on behalf of the new forest.

Finally, Brighter Than the Sun and Brighter Still felt they had no choice but to accompany their herds, for it was unthinkable that they should abandon them to their fate.

Then the peasants closed and bolted the gates, and they sent a delegation to Brahmadatta headed by an old man with white hair whose name was Old Man With White Hair, or Old for short. When the King had received them, Old stood up and said:

"Your Majesty. You are a king, and kings hunt. This we understand. You have our best wishes. But we have no extra men for scaring up deer and we have no extra children for your stray arrows. So we have built a big park, with waterfalls, trees and many other good things, and we have filled this park with two herds of deer led by wise leaders. We offer this park to you with respect and we hope that you will hunt there and nowhere else."

Brahmadatta was somewhat shocked by the bluntness of Old's speech. For a moment he thought perhaps he ought to have all their heads cut off. But he reflected that if he cut off their heads it might annoy their relatives and cause further trouble. "The next thing you know," he thought, "I shall have crowds of dirty people surrounding the palace smelling of garlic, their pockets stuffed with garbanzo beans. They will have torches and pitchforks . . ."

So, after drawing himself up in a regal pose and adopting a solemn air as if lost in meditation, he said, "We accept your offer. You are free to go."

So they went, and all the way home they laughed and sang and ate cold garbanzo beans. The older ones speculated about the cost of everything they had seen in the palace and the young ones swung their arms, told jokes and did king impersonations. Young and old, all were very happy that they still had their heads.

Next morning Brahmadatta went to inspect his new park. He found everything extremely well made. He began to blush as he thought of how much work the peasants had put into building it, and how anxious they must have been to get him out of their hair. As he walked about on his tour of inspection, he saw plenty of deer poking their heads out of the bushes. This was encouraging. Suddenly, as he rounded a bend in a stream he saw a magnificent stag standing and looking up towards the top of a hill. He was of such an intense gold that Brahmadatta had to look away. "My goodness," he thought, "this deer is brighter than the sun!" Just as he was recovering his composure, another stag walked slowly into view over the crest of the hill. The rays of the early sun gleamed on his silver antlers and glowed in his amber eyes. His black hooves were as shiny as if he had dipped them in a pot of varnish. And the fire of his golden body lit up the entire park. Brahmadatta felt faint and had to kneel on the grass. "Is it possible?" he thought. "This deer is brighter still!" His attendants rushed up to him and gave him strong tea with toddy. After a few minutes he was able to walk back to the gate, where he gave, with as much dignity as he could, a little speech:

"The park is acceptable to us, and we shall hunt here as often as it pleases us. The two golden deer, however, are hereby granted safety by me, and I forbid anyone to harm them. They are, after all, kings, and kings should not be harmed."

After that, Brahmadatta went every day to the park to hunt, surrounded by attendants and visiting dignitaries. Large amounts of rice wine were consumed, and wagers were made. Few of the hunters were marksmen, and the carnage was great. The deer, unable to flee the park, would run every which way in a panic with arrows flying around them, and for every deer killed outright three were wounded. Sick, thirsty, gut-shot and limping, they would wander about the park with wide eyes. Some lived; most did not.

Seeing what was happening, Brighter Still approached Brighter Than the Sun and said:

"Friend, this will not do. Our herds are being torn apart by pain, grief, lamentation and despair. Moreover, we cannot sustain these losses. We shall be destroyed. The loss of a single deer each day we can sustain, but no more. I have a proposal. Let us have our people take turns in going voluntarily to their deaths. One day a member of my herd will go and the next day a member of your herd will go. Lots will be drawn, and as they are drawn so will it be decided. When they go to the block there will be no panic and racing about. They will go in the knowledge that the decision is fair and that they go for the good of the herd. Straight to the stump of the great oak tree by the gate they will go, and when the King enters they will bow and lay down their head on the block. The meaning will be evident and the custom will quickly become established."

"Excellent," said Brighter Than the Sun. "This is a solution that is both reasonable and just."

When this plan was implemented the King was mystified, thrown off, put out. There was no question of his shooting a deer as it bowed before him or as it lay at his feet, and however much he shouted and waved his arms the deer would not flee. Finding the job of butcher beneath his dignity, he delegated the task to someone from his kitchen. So he continued to eat venison every day, but hunting deer in the park became impossible. Outside the park, he began to take out his frustration on everything in sight, using up more arrows than ever. Nothing that crawled, flew or swam was safe.

Now, one day a doe from the herd of Brighter Than the Sun approached him and said:

"Sir, today the lot of sacrifice has been drawn by me. If I were not pregnant I would be happy to take my turn. As it is, I request that you let my turn pass me by. If this is done the child and I will, in time, be able to offer the herd two deaths instead of one, and in the meantime the little one will have the pleasure of experiencing the world."

"I am afraid this is out of the question," said Brighter Than the Sun. "You know quite well how things work. Each deer draws a lot and each has an equal chance of going to the block. The system benefits us all and is scrupulously just. How could you think of violating it? How could I possibly throw your death onto the head of someone else? Go and take your turn."

But she did not. She went to Brighter Still and laid the matter before him. He thought for a moment and then said, "Very well, sister. I shall take your turn myself." And before she could reply he was gone.

When the butcher came and saw the golden deer lying at the block he was dazed, confused, at a loss. He sent someone to inform Brahmadatta, who soon arrived in his chariot, a crowd of hangers-on doing their best to keep up. Descending from the chariot, Brahmadatta said:

"King of the deer! What are you doing in this unclean place? I have granted you safety."

"Your Majesty, there is no cause for alarm. I am simply taking the place of a pregnant doe from our herds."

Brahmadatta did not know what to say. He was silent for some time. At last he said:

"King of the deer, you have taken for yourself the death that belongs to someone else and given someone else the life that belongs to you! In the stories told to me when I was a child I heard about this thing called self-sacrifice, but I have never seen it before, and the feelings I am feeling I have never felt before. Rise, I give you your life, and I give the doe her life as well!"

But Brighter Still did not move. He said:

"The doe and I have met with good fortune, Your Majesty, but what of the other deer in the park?"

"I give them their lives too!"

"Thank you, Your Majesty. But what of the deer in the forest?"

"I give them their lives!"

"Thank you, Your Majesty. The deer are now free from this danger. But what of the other four-footed creatures?"

"I give them their lives!"

"May all the four-footed creatures be happy, Your Majesty. But what of the birds who fly in the air?"

"I give them their lives!"

"And the fish who swim in the water?"

"I give them their lives!" laughed the King, and he began dancing.

"Their lives, their lives, I give them their lives," sang the King as he danced with one of his courtiers. "May they eat, may they drink, may they breathe," sang the King.

Then the Great Being got to his feet, and, after tossing his head so that his silver antlers sent beams of light in all directions, he was gone. That very day he and all the other deer, set free from the park, went home to the woods to live out the rest of their lives according to their wit and virtue.

This story is true. For justice is brighter than the sun, but mercy is brighter still. And the highest mercy is to sacrifice your own happiness for others.

May all beings be happy!

LORD KRISHNA AND KALIYA

RETOLD BY MIRA MISHRA

THERE ONCE LIVED in the great river Yamuna a mighty serpent named Kaliya.

One day Kaliya was commanded—in no uncertain terms—by the powerful man-bird Garuda to leave his native home of Ramanaka Dwipa. Garuda, an ancient foe of snakes, told Kaliya that if he were ever to return home again, he would surely meet his death. So the serpent moved to Vrindaban, which means "a forest of basil trees." Vrindaban was a place from which Garuda himself had been banished, because of some misdeed in a previous life.

Thus began the tyrannical rule of Kaliya who, in his arrogance and ignorance, without ever thinking of anyone else's happiness, began to take control of the river and the surrounding forest. Kaliya possessed formidable power. He was able to spout great quantities of poisonous venom—the smell of it alone caused peacocks to keel over and die.

Not just birds, but also cows, and even cowherds.

Upon hearing this, Lord Krishna came to the forest with his brother Balram and with one loving glance he revived the dead.

Then he joined in a game of ball with the other cowherds. He put aside his crown of peacock feathers and climbed up a Kadamba tree on the bank of the river. He reached up to catch a high toss of the ball but suddenly it fell into a cesspool of the river—in which the mighty serpent lived.

Hissing and spouting venom, the evil snake rose up and grabbed the ball. The cowherds all went into shock. And, to add to their dismay, they saw Lord Krishna jump in after the ball. A fierce battle began.

A gopi, or milkmaid, ran to tell Lord Krishna's mother, Yashoda, of the great battle ensuing between him and the giant serpent. Filled with terror and anxiety, Yashoda ran to the river and begged Lord Krishna to come out and forget about the ball. She appealed to him through tears—for everyone thought that he would surely die.

But little did the serpent know that the youthful boy he had wrapped his mighty coils around was really the Supreme Lord Himself—the mightiest avatar of the great god Vishnu. As the serpent tightened his grip around him, Lord Krishna enlarged his body to such an extent that the coils slackened like airless tires, and in a moment all his might was reduced to huffing and puffing.

So, knowing the Truth, the wives of the once powerful serpent came running, and surrounded Lord Krishna who had, by now, completely subdued the serpent and was standing atop him, dancing the great dance of Bharat-Natyam and playing his flute melodiously.

The wives of the serpent prayed to Lord Krishna, touched his feet respectfully and begged him to pardon their husband. Their plea was that, since Kaliya was just a snake, what else could he do if not frighten and poison everyone with his venom? *What's a snake to do?* they argued.

. . . Of course the ever-compassionate Lord Krishna understood and forgave Kaliya. Lord Krishna then told the serpent to go back to Ramanaka Dwipa and live there—without fear of reprisal from Garuda.

Bowing his one hundred and ten heads gratefully, the humbled serpent returned home with his wives and went on to become a worshipper of Lord Krishna.

THE CHOLA KING

RETOLD BY TIM WYNNE-JONES

THE BELL AT THE ENTRANCE to the palace could never have been said to jingle prettily like the little charms a princess might wear on her wrist or dangling from an ear; it did not ring out joyously like the instruments played by the courtly orchestra; nor did it peal like the bells that proclaimed a holiday or called the people to a feast; it did not even gravely toll in the manner of temple bells. The bell at the entrance to the palace boomed like something that had come from a great distance, the centre of the starry universe, perhaps, or, at the very least, the centre of the earth. *Boooooom.* A deeply melodious earthquake.

It did not sound often. And like an earthquake, however distant, its sound was not a welcome thing.

The old King awoke from a deep sleep, his head ringing. He shook it. The shattered bits of a rather shapely dream clattered about in the bottom of his brain pan. He was just trying to sort through the shards to find out the specific nature of the dream when his man-servant charged into the royal bedchamber desperately trying not to look weary or annoyed, both of which he evidently was.

"Do you dream?" the King asked him as the servant bustled about getting his large, sleepy body clothed.

"Don't have time," mumbled the servant. "But if Your Majesty wishes . . ."

"Do I have so much power?" said the King, obediently slipping his feet into his sandals.

"You are all powerful," said his servant, straightening the folds of the kingly robes with a not very gentle tug here and there.

"I am not, you know," said the King, impatiently waving aside his servant's ministrations. "All powerful, I mean." Even now the waves of sound from the mighty bell at the gate washed against the walls of his dimly lit chambers in the thin morning air, calling his most urgent attention.

"If you mean that you are slave to that bell," said the servant standing back to see if the King was presentable, "perhaps you should have a word with the fellow who hoisted it to so lofty a position."

The King loved this about his servant. He had heard that other kings were likely to have a man's head cut off for such impertinence, but he found it bracing. He had thought of promoting the servant to royal fool, but that would have forced him to be funny upon demand and so, wisely, he had kept him on as his personal valet, raising his salary but not so much as to make the man really happy. He did not want his attendant chirping.

"Not even the birds are up," said the King.

"It's the bell, Your Majesty. We shall find the royal courtyard strewn with their poor stunned little bodies come the morning."

And on that droll note the King followed his servant from the room, chuckling to himself until a yawn overcame him.

It was a long walk from the royal chambers in the tower by the gardens to the palace gates, but by the time the royal litter-bearers—shirt-tails flapping, head-dresses askew—caught up with the King, he was waking up and rather enjoying the stroll. He was trying to glue back together the pieces of his disrupted dream. Such fragile things, dreams. He was also rather excited. Someone had rung the bell.

Not knowing what else to do, the four strong, young litter-bearers fell in behind their master, at a suitable distance, carrying his elaborately curtained conveyance, empty though it might be, and feeling foolish.

The thing is, nobody was entirely sure yet what to do when the royal earthquake boomed out. It had only been in place a while. Protocol had not been established, and since the bell seldom rang, there never seemed any urgency to creating one. That is, until it happened again.

The courtyard was filled with townspeople gathering below the rampart wall, awaiting the royal appearance. Cynics among them were betting he would not show. The fearful were prepared for the worse. Others cursed the great, grey monster and scanned the crowd for the culprit who had dared to sound it. Dawn, herself, seemed to have sensed the occasion, though she was in no hurry to make a full appearance. Walking along an eastern bulwark, the King could see a light on in her room on the distant horizon of the sea. He imagined her servings girls dressing her in robes of shimmering saffron. Taking their time. He wondered if Dawn suffered impertinent talk from her menials? Probably not. Oh to catch just a glimpse of her shimmering flesh. Now there was *real* power.

Then he emerged onto the rampart below which his people gathered by torchlight. In another age a torchlight gathering in the small hours might have meant an insurrection. The King shuddered at the memory for he had seen the people take up arms on more than one occasion, although not in his reign, and he had seen what inevitably happened to them. That, after all, was the very reason he'd elevated the great bell to its present use. Once there was true Justice, revolution would become a thing of the past.

There was a stone chair convenient to the bell. The King sat. It wasn't much as thrones go—it was actually cold and wet with dew— but it was a signal of sorts; the mob quieted in anticipation.

The court herald arrived on the scene about then, still labouring over the broach of his official court herald sash. He was a little out of breath but covered it well.

"The People's Bell has been sounded," he proclaimed. "Step forward bell-ringer without fear of punishment and state your complaint to His Majesty." Perhaps no one but the King noticed the omission in the set text, which he had written himself. It was supposed to be "state your request or complaint." But perhaps the slip was understandable. Who, in his right mind, would have dared to ring the bell before cockcrow with a request?

Then a poor old fellow stepped forward and with great temerity lamented the circumstances that had provoked him to ring the bell.

"The revelry, Your Highness," he said. "For three nights in a row. Such revelry in the east wing of the palace that none of us who live below can get a wink of sleep." Neighbours, seeing no guards rushing out to gore the protester, stepped forward murmuring agreement. "Three nights." "Awful hullabaloo."

Now the King was surprised at this. He knew of no party. He liked parties. But then an advisor whispered in his ear that the prince had indeed been beguiling away the night in regular fashion lately with some of his cronies and a rather large assortment of wenches. Not to mention beer.

"If it were some festival," said the bell-ringer. "I mean to say, if I knew for certain it would come to an *end*."

The King looked around him. The prince was nowhere among his retinue. He asked the herald to call for silence.

Sure enough, when everybody had stopped murmuring and shuffling about, the blare of a party could distinctly be heard. There was laughing and music and song and the odd scream, presumably of delight.

"It might seem a small matter, Your Highness, but I am at my wit's end. I rang the bell knowing that death itself could not be worse than this."

"Surely a sleeping draught would be sufficient," whispered the King's man-servant.

The King smiled. He had a good smile and there was very little room left on his face for solemnity. The change in expression did not go unnoticed below. Suddenly a young woman burst from the crowd and stood next to the old man.

"It is not my place to speak," she said, "but my father has left out of his complaint the most unpleasant part."

The King reassumed a sober expression.

"A drunkard fell or jumped from the window. He broke clear through our roof. Who will pay for this?"

The King was wide awake now. He was thinking the drunkard must certainly have paid for it and dearly too.

"Is this true?" he demanded. But when the roof in question was pointed out to him, he could see the damage even in the dim light of early dawn.

He didn't need his advisors to tell him this was an important test, though they buzzed around him in an obliging swarm.

"He's known around the market as an incorrigible whiner."

His own son—his only son.

"I see a fair number of smirks down there. They're playing on your good grace."

Just a boy after all, spoilt, headstrong.

"The prince will one day be their king. Best not to raise their hopes."

Why did the Queen have to go and die?

"Or excite their craving. See how already they abuse the power you have so generously given them. They'll make a fool of you, if you let them."

The King waved his advisors away and closed his eyes. He was finding it hard to think clearly. This dream of his—this notion of Justice— there were still many wrinkles to it. Fairness was at the heart of it. What was fair? A new roof, certainly. Beyond that? Then it came to him: a party. A—how many nights?—three-night party. Paid for by the King.

"Justice must be appropriate," pronounced the King, quite pleased with this turn of phrase considering it had come along extemporaneously while sitting on his wet bottom at an extremely early hour in the morning.

The crowd in the square looked stunned with the news, the bell-ringer quite ashen.

The King turned to his man-servant. "What do you think they expected?"

The prince was outraged.

"Has it occurred to you that the peasants' shacks lean against the very walls of the palace? That we are supporting them, literally?"

The King was, at last, having breakfast—avocados in cream and sugar—in his favourite throne room. "Actually," he said, "that has occurred to me."

The prince scowled at him. "They are an eyesore," he said.

"The peasants?"

"The shacks. I will have them torn down when I am king."

The King quickly took a sip of tea to stop himself from answering his petulant son too precipitously. He was drinking more tea than usual these days. He placed the golden teacup down on the little rosewood table beside the throne. He turned the handle of the cup so that all the tea things made a pleasing pattern on the tray.

"That is good news," he said, much to his son's surprise. "New housing is dreadfully expensive, but I'm glad you consider it a priority."

The boy stamped his foot. He wore bells around his ankles. They tinkled. They tinkled a lot lately, thought the King, sighing. It was a fashion he did not much care for.

The boy marched up and took a mango from the fruit bowl on the table. He peeled it with a sharp knife, tore at the orange flesh disconsolately. He's so young, thought his father, admiring the boy's dashing features and almost hairless cheek. How difficult it is for him.

Then, *tinkle, tinkle.*

"It's that damnable bell!"

"It is rather loud," said the King.

The boy threw the mango skin on the floor. "Father, stop playing games with me. I'm not a child any more. You know perfectly well what I mean. Yes, it is loud. Precisely because it was meant to sit in a tower up in the hills where it could be heard throughout the kingdom. That was what your great-great-grandfather had in mind. An extraordinary bell to be rung on high holidays and royal weddings to remind the people of the all-powerful ruler who watched over them and to whom they owed obeisance. Lest they forget."

The King mopped his lips with a large red napkin. He stared unhappily at the lacerated mango skin on the floor. "You have learned your history lessons well," he said. "And one day, dear boy, the tutors will tell their charges of the King who had the bell moved down to the gates of the palace lest *he* forget."

"Pah!" said the prince and marched back and forth like a caged tiger. His father watched the boy's feet, waiting for him to step on the mango skin and go for a loop—just about serve him right. But he missed it again and again. The prince had an annoying way of lifting and lowering each foot like a parade horse or like the Emperor of Rathu Isso, a red-faced tyrant of a fellow who, although very regal, the King did not much care for.

"Pah!"

"You can 'pah!' all you want," said the King. "I had a dream. There was an enormously tall coconut tree and—"

"You and your dreams!" cried the boy. The King clamped his mouth shut. The boy was exasperating, to be sure; but it did not do to exasperate him further. The prince had his own dreams. Leopards and women as lithe as leopards; the sharp weapons of the chase; dreams of conquest. The dreams of any ordinary youth. The prince, however, was not an ordinary youth. The entire kingdom, the resplendent island, would one day be his. This was not a matter about which the King could afford to banter with, much less alienate, his son.

"I will have justice for my people," said the King. "Even unto the most humble of them. That is what the bell is for. Appropriate justice. I am not even sure what that is, not yet, let alone how it is to be brought about. That is what the bell is for. It will speak to me. I will listen. It is a grand experiment."

"And if it rings every day?"

"Then we will all go quite deaf, won't we."

The boy crossed his slim arms and pouted. The King searched the fruit bowl for a banana. It had been a wearying morning.

"So," said the prince, "I suppose we shall have parties all the time now."

"Oh, I doubt that," said the King, his mouth full of banana. "Partying is very taxing." He was quite proud of the pun but the prince showed no signs of having got it, overtaxed, as he was, from his own partying.

"Every time someone feels like knocking off work, kicking up their heels at *our* expense, they'll trump up some complaint expecting the King will come through. Why don't you just hand over the keys to the royal coffers, let them cart it all away."

The King nodded. He understood the boy's concerns. He seldom had nightmares but this was one of them. He didn't really much like peasants. He didn't like the idea of their traipsing through the palace carting things away. They smelled of fish and spoke too loudly and their teeth were crooked. He had heard them through his window often enough when the royal chambers were near the gate—where his son's apartment was now. He was not proud of having moved to the tower above the garden, but he rationalized it this way: if he slept better, he'd be a more merciful ruler. Also, when he slept, he dreamt quite marvellously and sometimes the peasantry of his resplendent island peopled his dreams. They smelled just fine, in his dreams. And their teeth were always straight.

"We are finding, my son, that Justice is a very difficult business. For everyone. Our subjects will learn in time but only when we have learned."

His son glared at him. "And in the meantime, where do you think these subjects of yours are going to learn about self-restraint?" With that, he turned on his very shapely heel and left the room tinkling the whole way.

Months passed without the bell ringing again. Everything was not well in the kingdom. There was unrest in one of the northern provinces, but peace continued to reign within range of the huge and, for the time being, silent bell. After the three nights of festivity brought about by the last complaint, people were not quick to seek royal redress. They were learning, the King hoped. And he had plans for other such bells, so that the whole of the island could be brought within a rope's length of Justice. Peace, he was quite convinced, could not help but thrive in a land where the King was everywhere accessible. Mind you, his uplifting dreams did not exactly explain how this omnipresence was to be accomplished.

Meanwhile, within the palace, the prince steamed and bubbled like sour soup. The King had always thought the boy quite bright and welcomed the opportunity to joust with him about his Great Experiment. But the King began to suspect that his son's argument was not entirely his own. The King recognized the voices of certain disgruntled advisors: Vantakolu, for instance, a misshapen but otherwise hardy minister of the court, and the lugubrious Babath, both of whom were shrewd and both of whom had been outraged at the bell's being moved from its distant hillside and installed so achingly close to home. Certain phrases that clattered from the princely mouth bore their mark, unless the King missed his guess. Lately, Vantakolu and Babath had shown—or seemed to—a certain restraint in condemning the issue so dear to the King's heart. But perhaps, thought the King, they felt they had found a better path to his ear? The King told himself that, in any case, it was good that the future king was beginning to listen to his elders. A king must have ministers. But he was perturbed all the same.

Then one night the bell boomed again. There was a banquet at the time. The prince had been on a hunt and had bagged a magnificent leopard, the skin of which he had thrown across the back of his chair at the banquet table. He was regaling the dinner party with details of the hunt and was just getting to the scary part, where the jaw of the leopard was closing around his neck, when the dinner dishes started to rattle. *Boooooom.* The bell sounded positively mournful. Several courtiers cast doleful glances at the King; some were out and out hostile towards him—none more so than the prince, the spotlight having been snatched away from his performance.

So the assembled court could not have been more surprised to find, upon gathering on the rampart above the gate, a cow below them with the bell-rope still in her crooked, brown teeth.

The court herald was clearing his throat to begin his prepared speech when someone thumped him on the back. "Oh my," he said.

"Dinner," said one of the court wags, and everyone had a good laugh. Even the King was amused and, quite frankly, relieved. It was all a mistake, a farcical distraction. Ammunition for his detractors, perhaps, but really only a false alarm. Some of the dinner party, including the prince, started back immediately towards the dining chambers when suddenly the cow spoke and the party stopped in its tracks.

"It is my calf," said the cow.

"What?" said the King.

"He is dead."

"Dear, dear," said the King. Since he had never spoken to a cow before, he was a little slow on the uptake. "I'm sorry to hear that." He could hear the stifled laughter of his dinner guests. This was really rather too much.

"He was killed, Your Majesty, crushed under the wheels of a chariot." The King flinched. "A ghastly kind of death," he said.

"It sounds like bull to me," murmured someone, which started a new wave of snickers and chortles.

The cow persevered. "A chariot driven by your son," she said.

The crowd was silenced. The King turned to his boy with a grave expression on his face. The prince rushed forward.

"It was an accident!" he said, angrily. "For God's sake, Father."

"I'm sure," said the King with a sinking feeling in his heart. "I'm sure that it was not intentional."

The cow, nodding sadly, lowered her head. "I understand."

"The boy will apologize," said the King, turning to his son.

"To a cow!" he said. His eyes flashed with contempt. "Is this supposed to be a joke?"

"No," said the King. "It most assuredly is not." A crowd had gathered in the court below. The King looked down upon them. He saw a lick of curry on one boy's chin, a half-eaten pappadam in a man's hand. They had been at supper, too. They stood in expectant silence. They had never heard a cow speak, let alone to a king. And now the King would speak. But he could not. The silence lengthened.

"Pah!" said the prince. "I suppose there will have to be an appropriate punishment. How about we arrange for me to be run over by a chariot. Would that be fair, mother cow?"

The cow lowered her head. How tired she looked, thought the King. How dusty from her great walk to the palace, for the prince had been hunting many miles away.

The King put his arm around his son's shoulder and looked him square in the eye. He saw his dead queen there. He spoke in the feeblest of whispers, not a command, but a heartfelt plea. "Apologize, my child."

The prince's jaw gaped open. He looked away and then back at his friends. The King could not see his son's expression, but he saw a reflection of the boy's derision on their faces. Their smirks, however, disappeared quickly enough as they saw the clouds gathering on the kingly brow. The boy turned his gaze back to his father. "Oh, Daddy, how displeased you look. How about we throw a party instead. Isn't that what we did last time? We get mother cow here to gather up all her bovine friends. It will be a kind of a wake. What do you say."

There was a hush now. The King felt quite dizzy. His man-servant came quickly to his aid, helped him to his stone seat. Even warmed by the sun it was a most uncomfortable throne.

His voice was subdued when he made his decree; his audience had to strain to hear. But they did hear, even those in the very back of the crowd below. The boy was to be taken away to a cell, there to await the same fate that had befallen the calf. The cow turned sadly away and headed homeward. She had a bell around her neck. It jangled most mournfully.

The advisors spoke as a unified group without apparent dissent. "This justice you have dreamt up, Your Majesty, it must be written down for all to hear. It must be organized, given a coherent shape. It is too oner-ous a responsibility for one man, even a man of great vision, to mete out on the spur of the moment."

A month now had passed since the death of the King's son. No one dared touch the rope of the mighty bell at the gate. Some were sure the King was a lunatic and feared what he might do to the next bell-ringer. But most of his subjects were too filled with sadness. In the King's loss they saw the dreadful size of it. Justice, it seemed, was no party.

"Your Majesty?"

He had not answered his royal advisory board. "Yes, yes," he said.

"There must be rules, Sire."

His dreams had deserted him but he found himself suddenly recall-ing a dream of some months earlier. A very shapely dream that had been interrupted. The shape of it was a bell. He had seen a bell being made once, a lovely bronze bell. Once the bell had been poured into its mold of clay and horse dung and buried in the sand to set, it had been dragged out and hung where a monk with a very fine ear and an incred-ibly sharp knife had scraped away at the inside of the bell to tune it. Scrape and strike, scrape and strike until the tone was just right.

"Rules?" said the King. "Yes, I suppose so."

THE RESTING HILL

RETOLD BY GRIFFIN ONDAATJE

AN OLD MAN AND HIS GRANDDAUGHTER came walking down the country road. As they climbed a small hill, where a tall palmyra tree stood, the old man slowed down.

"Let's rest a minute," he said.

He took a green mango from a basket and bit into it.

The girl took a mango also.

The old man sat down beside the road, and pointed at the palmyra tree up on the hill. "See that palmyra there?" he said. "And the way there's a wide dip to the ground, as if a giant rock had fallen there?" he asked, chewing quickly.

"Yes," the girl said, a little impatiently. She was tired of walking so slowly with her grandfather. "That tree's been there forever."

"No. There was another tree there—a long time ago. An elephant had to wait beside it a very long time, you know. Have you heard this one before?"

The girl didn't answer. So the man began his tale . . . .

Once there was an old elephant-tamer who lived here in the north, near Kumulanai.

His name was Velappanikkar and his wife's name was Ariyaatthai. Velappanikkar was once the best elephant-tamer in the kingdom. He could tame any elephant because he was very brave and patient. After a long life of elephant taming he retired and built a house beside this road, a mile from here, and lived a peaceful life gardening with his wife.

One morning Velappanikkar and Ariyaatthai were working in their garden when they heard a terrible crash like thunder. People started screaming, and then another crash followed and then more screams. The sounds were coming from across the paddy field and Velappanikkar ran out of the garden to see what had happened.

What is it? called Ariyaatthai.

What it was, was a giant elephant on the far side of the field. It had knocked down a small house and chased away several farmers who ran splashing into the paddy fields. Their oxen were running as well—hauling plows behind them.

In anger, the elephant turned towards a nearby tree and ran forward at full speed, smashing it. The elephant stood there motionless, and started to push against the tree until the tree bent back suddenly and fell over, its roots torn out of the ground.

Velappanikkar watched all this. He'd never seen an elephant do that before. Coming to his senses, he turned and walked over to the tool-shed and pulled out a rope and went out into the field. As he began to run, a thought came to him—a thought he had never had before: perhaps this elephant is one I cannot tame.

Velappanikkar looked again and saw the elephant was now disappearing into the forest, but he continued across the field to see if the farmers were hurt.

The grandfather interrupted himself and took a bite of his mango. He chewed for some time.

"An untamed elephant who attacks people for no reason, such as this one did, is a rogue elephant," he said slowly. "And as you know, a rogue elephant is very dangerous—impossible to tame. And in those days an elephant-tamer who failed to subdue a rogue elephant in less than thirty days was killed."

He glanced at his granddaughter, who seemed to be listening, and continued:

Sure enough, a few days later, the King sent the following message:

"Velappanikkar, catch this rogue elephant at once. You have one month."

Now, Velappanikkar was retired but the King had given his orders. Velappanikkar went back inside the house. He went into the bedroom and lay down. He felt weak. He remembered how the elephant had smashed that tree and how his confidence fell away from him.

Ariyaatthai went and sat beside him. She had never seen Velappanikkar this worried.

Three weeks later the King's messenger came again and asked if Velappanikkar had tamed the elephant. Ariyaatthai met him at the door:

"My husband's fallen ill," *she said.* "Please find someone else to catch this elephant."

But the messenger wouldn't listen. He shook his head and repeated the King's orders.

Ariyaatthai went over to Velappanikkar who was lying sick in bed. He hadn't been out of bed in weeks. His strength was fading and he couldn't bring himself to eat. Ariyaatthai was worried that he might be dying.

She realized something had to be done. I'll try to catch this elephant, *she thought. So, after dusk, she went to the shed and took the rope and put it over her shoulder, then she went quietly out the front gate . . . .*

The grandfather patted the road with his palm: "She stepped onto this very same road."

He stood up and stretched his legs and pointed down the road with the half-eaten mango in his hand. "It was just a sandy cart road in those days but it went deep into the jungle. It was here that Ariyaatthai walked along . . . ."

Though it was dark the bright moonlight made the road's tracks glow like elephant tusks. Up ahead the tracks curved and disappeared into the forest. Soon Ariyaatthai was in that darkness which she and Velappanikkar had only seen from their porch.

Yet she wasn't as afraid as she thought she'd be, and there was a strange peacefulness to the forest around her. Stars were all over the sky—so many that she stopped for several minutes to admire them. She walked underneath the stars for several more miles tilting her head to look up at the sky. Then she came to a small pond and stepped off the road to sit there and rest. There were hoof prints of deer and water-buffalo who had come to drink, and among them were enormous round elephant footprints pressed deep into the muddy slope. She was sure the elephant would come back that night to drink.

She waited . . . .

The night was completely silent around her, except for the steady chant of crickets. Once, their chant seemed to grow unusually loud, and then they stopped altogether—and didn't start again—and the silence grew very frightening. Ariyaatthai stopped breathing and listened for some time. It was as if the forest had taken a step closer to her. The crickets finally resumed their chanting, and Ariyaatthai relaxed and felt courage return. Yet she knew her heart was beating fast now.

Eventually dawn arrived. Ariyaatthai had stayed awake all night, and now stood up slowly and turned to go back home.

The sand on the road was bright pink in the morning light, soft and cool under her feet, and she almost slept as she walked.

But, a mile from home, the rogue elephant suddenly appeared.

It was standing only a hundred yards away—its huge ears waving in the air like heavy carpets—its giant feet shifting, stirring up the dust. Before Ariyaatthai could move it trumpeted and charged towards her.

The grandfather stepped back from the middle of the road. "This is the frightening part," he said. He stared up the road as if he saw something, then he took a bite of his mango.

"Go on," said the girl anxiously.

The old man stood there, chewing. "Well then . . ."

The road began to shake under Ariyaatthai's feet. But she stood there, planted to the ground. She thought of her husband, Velappanikkar, and even though she was afraid for both their lives, she still couldn't move. She felt she had nowhere to run and she could only stare at the terrible image of this charging elephant . . .

. . . and—as if the elephant were charging through water—grass by the road brushed back like reeds in a river, and even coconut trees seemed to lean back slightly, the birds disappeared and there were no monkeys in the trees.

When the elephant was only fifty feet away Ariyaatthai still didn't move. Her bare feet stayed flat on the ground and her legs seemed to be held, like trees, to the earth. She began to remember all the things she loved and it felt as if her memories came rushing up to her through roots in the soil. She was about to cry out. But then, in the same moment, she made herself take a step forward.

She lifted up her arms and held open her hands and showed the rope to the elephant. She closed her eyes . . . .

"You see, she knew the elephant was wild and that a rogue elephant can never be tamed, but she still hoped to communicate her own sorrow somehow."

All of a sudden the wild elephant stopped.

It came close to Ariyaatthai—its face only inches away from hers. Dust rose around her. She opened her eyes and the elephant was there, glaring at her. Air poured down on her face in long warm breaths, as if it were the winds inside a cave lightly touching her skin. The elephant was just standing there, right in front of her—staring. They both stood still, not sure what would happen next. Ariyaatthai slowly raised her hand to touch the elephant's forehead. It turned away from her and walked up the road to a low hill where a palmyra tree stood. There it stopped and stood still, under the tree.

It wasn't afraid when Ariyaatthai walked up and tied one end of her rope to the palmyra tree and the other end to his foot. If it had wanted to, the elephant could have broken the rope, but it was tired of running now.

The grandfather took a last bite of his mango and tossed it into the bushes.

"What happened then?" asked the girl.

"Well . . . no one came back to untie the elephant. Ariyaatthai went home but it turned out Velappanikkar had passed away during the night—and she herself died of grief.

"So the elephant was left standing there on the hill . . . that's why there's a mark there, because he waited so patiently for Ariyaatthai to come back and untie him."

The girl was quiet, wanting to hear more. Her grandfather had a way of making up stories when he wanted to rest during the long walk home. He finished stories when he was ready to go.

She watched as he lovingly selected another mango from the basket.

"All right then, let's go home," he said, and he tossed the mango over to the palmyra tree, as an offering.

THE DEER, THE TORTOISE AND THE KAERALA BIRD

RETOLD BY J.B. DISANAYAKA

ONCE UPON A TIME, there was a deer. He lived under a tree near a pond. In the pond lived a tortoise and on that tree was a kaerala bird. All three were good friends.

One day, a hunter set a trap just below the tree where these animals met. At dawn, as the deer set out to go looking for food, he was caught in the trap. He tried to get out of it but he could not. He was shaken by a fear of death and began to cry. His friends heard the cry and they came over to see the deer. The bird saw the deer trapped in a snare and told his friend the tortoise, "Friend tortoise, you have teeth in your mouth. Therefore you had better bite the rope that is tied to the trap. While you do that I will prevent the hunter from coming here." As the tortoise began to bite the rope, the bird flew towards the hut where the hunter lived. He settled on a tree in front of the hut and waited there all night.

The hunter woke up the next morning and set off to see if he had caught any animal in his trap. As the hunter stepped out of his hut, the bird cried loudly and flew down, making his wings touch the hunter's head. The hunter was angry because it is a bad omen to hear the cry of a kaerala bird when someone leaves the house to go somewhere. He said, "What a wretched bird!"—and went back to his hut.

The bird thought thus: "The hunter will not leave his hut again from the front door. So I will now wait at the back door." So he flew over to the back yard and waited there for the hunter to come out. The hunter also thought thus: "Last time I went out of the front door, and then I met this wretched bird. Now I will avoid him and go out by the back door." Thus thinking, he left the hut by the back door. As soon as he stepped out of the hut he heard the bird cry, flying just above him. He returned to the hut again and thought, "I will not go just now but I will wait till the bird leaves."

And he waited for several hours. When he left again the bird did not cry, but it flew back and told the deer that the hunter was on his way now. Luckily, at that moment, the tortoise had just finished gnawing through all but one of the strands of rope. The tortoise's mouth was bleeding, and he was lying down exhausted.

The deer saw the hunter approaching and ran into the jungle, freeing himself from the last strand with one leap. The bird flew up and settled on a high branch in a tree. The tortoise, however, could not move and the hunter caught him and put him inside his bag and left it hanging on the fence.

The deer watched what was happening and was sorry that the tortoise who tried to help him was caught by the hunter. Forgetting about his wounded leg, the deer ran forward through the bushes and appeared in front of the hunter. When the hunter had seen him, the deer ran away again and the hunter followed, certain that the deer could be caught easily. But the deer leapt and disappeared and so the hunter was left behind and he lost his way in the jungle. The deer ran in a wide circle and came back to where the bag was, and tore it open with its antlers. The tortoise dropped heavily to the ground.

"Tortoise—my friend! You had better get into the water and swim down. And you, kaerala bird, my friend—you should fly to a tree farther away." So saying, the deer ran into the wild forest. When the hunter returned none of the animals were to be seen.

WATER UNDER A ROCK

RETOLD BY GEORGE WOODCOCK

LONG AGO IN THE KINGDOM of Benares in India, the Buddha-to-be was born into the family of a rich merchant. He adopted his father's calling and eventually, when he grew up, he was entrusted to take large caravans of goods on long journeys into strange places and there to sell and buy for the family's profit. At length he was given charge of a caravan of five hundred oxcarts, with its guides and its escort of armed outriders.

He came on the way to a desert that stretched for hundreds of miles. Its sand was so fine that it ran like water through the fingers of a closed fist. When the sun rose it became as hot as a bed of burning embers of charcoal, and nobody—man or beast—could walk upon it. Neither water nor food, firewood nor shelter were to be found in these hundreds of miles, so that all such supplies had to be taken with them. The caravan travelled by night, starting off as soon as the sand cooled after sunset, as it does quickly in desert climates. As the five hundred carts straggled over several miles, each group of carts had a drummer playing constantly so that the other carts would know where to follow during the night. And right at the head of the caravan, in a separate cart with a couch to sit on, rode the man they called the desert-pilot, who directed the whole column by his reading of the stars in the unpolluted skies of long ago. Beside him rode a man on a camel, carrying the flag of the caravan. At dawn the carts would form a circular encampment; the awnings would be put out and the men would sleep in the shadow of their carts.

After many days, the time came when they stopped at dawn and the desert-pilot said they were only a few miles from the city on the far edge of the desert that was their destination. To lessen the load on their exhausted oxen, the young merchant ordered that the remnant of their fuel and water be discarded.

But the next night's journey, instead of being a few miles only, seemed never to end, and dawn found them in a strange part of the desert. Tired after many nights of sleepless watching, the desert-pilot had fallen asleep in his cart, and now awoke with a loud cry: "Turn the carts!" They camped in that strange spot. There was no water to be seen and they had poured their own away. The men slunk under the carts to lie in despair. The oxen lowed grievously. And the Buddha-to-be said to himself, "I must find water or we shall surely die!"

So, before the sun began to rise high, he wandered outside the camp, looking for signs, and eventually he came to a clump of desert grass, and knew that there must be water underneath. So he called for men to come with spades, and dig down beneath the clump of grass.

Tired and thirsty as they were, they dug with the energy of despair, passing the soil up in baskets on ropes. They dug down sixty feet, and then their spades rang against a great rock that blocked off the hole. The young merchant clambered down one of the ropes and knelt to put his ear to the rock. Faintly he could hear the sound of water flowing. So he called on one of the strongest of his young men to come down with a great iron hammer and break the rock.

The first young man failed, and so did a second, but the third finally broke the stone and the water came rushing up so fast—as high as a palm tree—that he barely escaped as they pulled him up on the ropes.

They all drank and washed immediately. They chopped up their spare axles and yokes and cooked their rice and fed their cattle. And as the sun set they hoisted a flag beside the well as a sign for other travellers. And then the drums beat to resume their journey. This time the young merchant travelled with the desert-pilot to make sure he did not sleep again.

They reached their destination after a long night's journey. In the city they bartered their goods for four times their cost, and returned over the desert without further mishap to enjoy their prosperity.

TWO FRIENDS BY THE VILLU

RETOLD BY RANJINI OBEYESEKERE

IN THE SOUTH-EAST CORNER of the lovely island of Lanka was a forest. The trees in this forest were tall with wide spreading branches. Green vines clung to their trunks and laced themselves among the high branches. Yellow hornbills, green parrots and black-headed golden orioles flew in and out of the leaves. Hordes of chattering monkeys played in the trees and the brambles.

In the middle of the forest was a large *villu* or pond. Lush grass grew at the edges of the villu and in the evening all the animals of the forest gathered here to drink. The big, slow elephants would bring their babies and sit for hours in the cool water lazily plucking up turfs of grass. Hordes of deer would come quickly, nervously drink at the pond and then disappear. Water-buffalo wallowed in the water all day and sometimes all night and all next day too. Occasionally a leopard would walk proudly to the water, look around as if it all belonged to him, drink and slowly walk away. Pond herons and pink-breasted storks perched stiffly on the bare branches of dead trees.

At the edge of the villu in a glade of green grass there lived a rabbit. Her name was Hahami. In the forest beyond lived a fox. His name was Narinayide. Each evening as the fox came down to drink Hahami would be contentedly nibbling the lush grass. But she would always stop eating to exchange a word of greeting as he passed. Soon the two became friends. Often Narinayide would drag his piece of half-eaten meat to where Hahami sat nibbling and the two of them would eat their meal together. They would then go down to the water together to drink and would sit by a rock near the villu talking and talking, until the moon showed her face in the sky and the water. Only then would they part to go about their business, or to sleep.

The animals in this forest lived happily. There was always plenty to eat and plenty of water to drink, because the villu never dried up; not even in the dry season when all the rivers and streams in the forest turned into damp tracks of pebbles and rocks.

But one year the rains did not break. The hot sun burned the forest. The monsoon months came and went but no rain fell. The big trees with their spreading branches turned brown and shed their leaves. The vines drooped, dried up and slipped to the ground in masses of tangles. The glade around the villu was no longer green but a dull grey, caked into squares of hard mud and dust. Every day when the animals came to drink they had to walk farther and farther into the middle of the villu. Each day the water shrank. The monkeys were the first to leave. Their chattering ceased. Soon the elephants were no longer seen. They had moved to distant parts in search of water. The herds of deer got thinned out. Many died; some moved away. It was getting too dangerous for them as the water-hole got smaller and smaller. When the deer stopped coming, the leopard, now lean and scraggy, stopped coming too. Soon only the fox and the rabbit were left.

The two friends sat by the rock, looked up at the sky and shook their heads mournfully.

"Not a cloud in the sky, friend," said Hahami. "I am afraid it will not rain today, or tomorrow."

"Yes," said the fox gloomily. He was becoming increasingly morose and grumpy, and less and less talkative. There was little for him to eat in the forest, with the deer gone and the leopard, who used to catch them, gone. And how could he engage in conversation when all he heard was the rumbling in his stomach, telling him in no uncertain terms that he had not had food now for days.

"Soon there'll be only us two left in this forest," continued Hahami, trying to be cheerful. "But don't worry. Our villu is almost dry now but there is still a puddle in the middle and if I dig hard enough under it you and I will have enough water to live on till the rains come."

"Yes," said the fox. "But what will I eat?"

"You come with me, friend. There's still a few greens growing in nooks and crannies. I'll show you where to find them."

"I don't eat grasses," muttered Narinayide shortly. "Greens are good only for rabbits, not for me."

So the two friends sat staring at the sky and at the dry brown forest, with only the rumblings in Narinayide's stomach disturbing their unusual silence.

As they sat thus in the long hot evening, hunger and tiredness made the fox rather dizzy. His head began to spin and his eyes half closed. After a while he began to see, seated on the rock in front of him, not the thin, worn, friendly face of Hahami, but a sleek brown rabbit, juicy and tender, with long limbs and a soft fat stomach. Narinayide's eyes now narrowed to slits. The more he looked at the rabbit on the rock, the more his mouth watered for a juicy morsel of rabbit flesh.

"Well, I must be going, friend," said Hahami, depressed by the silence. Narinayide sat up with a jerk. He must have been dreaming. That was his old friend Hahami sitting there on the rock, not a tasty morsel of rabbit flesh. How could he have made such a mistake?

"I must be off too," he said a trifle apologetically. "I must see if I can find something to eat."

They each wandered off in search of food. That night the fox slept fitfully. He kept dreaming of rabbits—fat ones, short ones, brown ones, grey ones, all juicy and plump and oh so good to eat! When he woke up and looked around he realized, however, that he was alone in the forest and the only rabbit around was Hahami his friend.

As he walked all day, roaming the forest in search of food, he kept thinking of rabbits. Soon he was thinking of a rabbit—*the* rabbit—the only rabbit around. Finally, exhausted and starving, he sat under a tree and thought it through. He had to find food. There was nothing in the forest to eat. There was only one animal left and that was a rabbit, his friend. Therefore, if he had to have food he had to eat Hahami. But Hahami was his friend. How could he kill and eat his friend? But if he didn't eat her he would surely die. All through the hot dry afternoon Narinayide pondered the question.

Finally, as the sun went down he made his way to the usual meeting place at the villu. He decided to put the problem to Hahami. She was a sensible creature and a good friend and would surely not want to see him die. He would discuss the matter with her.

He arrived at the rock earlier than usual and greeted Hahami warmly when she made her appearance. Hahami came hopping up, glad that her friend's glum mood of the previous day had passed.

"Come here, Hahami. I have a big problem to discuss with you."

"What is it?" asked Hahami, settling herself in the shade of the rock and comfortably scratching her ear.

"You know there is a severe drought and famine in our forest," continued Narinayide.

"Yes, yes," nodded Hahami. "But by the mercy of the gods the rains will come soon."

"Who knows?" said the fox sarcastically. "The gods may not think about it till next year."

Hahami nodded mournfully, agreeing that in fact it might be so.

"Well," said Narinayide, continuing his speech. "This forest is bone dry. All the forest creatures are dead or gone away. Only you and I are left."

"Yes," said Hahami sadly, shaking her paws to clean the mud.

"Well you see, this is my problem. I'm starving. There's nothing to eat in the forest. The only living thing left to be eaten is you."

"But . . . but . . . but . . . ," stammered Hahami, staggered by the enormity of the problem. "But you can't do that . . . I'm your friend."

"That is precisely the problem," answered the fox. "However, if we could get into a fight, then I could get angry and eat you up. We won't be friends then and I won't feel so bad."

"But . . . but . . . ," stuttered Hahami, still suffering from shock. "What will we fight about?"

"Let's see," said the fox, tackling the problem now very enthusiastically. "How shall we set about it? Ah . . . . You see this rock where we sit every evening. Now I will sit on it and say, 'This rock is mine!' Then you stand there and say, 'No, it's mine!' We will argue about it and then we will fight and I will eat you up."

"Well . . . " Hahami hesitated, still rather confused and dumbfounded.

The fox now stood up on the rock, his ears upright, his tail taut. "This rock is *mine!*" he declared.

Hahami stood silent.

"Come on," said the fox. "Speak up. Say it's yours."

"It's . . . m-mine," stuttered Hahami not very convincingly.

"How dare you say that?" shouted the fox, working himself up into a rage. "How dare you, little *rabbit*, tell me, Narinayide, that this rock, on which I have sat every evening for as long as I can remember, belongs to you. It is mine. Mine I say! Do you hear? This rock is MINE!" and the fox snarled at Hahami, showing long, white, vicious teeth. The hairs on his back bristled with rage and expectation.

"Well . . . ," said Hahami, suddenly collecting her wits. "Well, friend, if you insist and say so, then the rock is yours and you may certainly have it." In a flash she vanished into her burrow and took great care never to come out again when her hungry friend was about.

THE VULTURE

RETOLD BY MICHAEL ONDAATJE

WHEN THE BODHISATTVA WAS being born, again and again, he emerged as many things. He was born as an eagle five times, once as a waterfowl, once as a jungle-cock, and four times as a peacock. This is the story of what happened when he was born as a vulture.

Once, in the middle of his vulture life, a storm rolled over India, taking a month to cross the whole country. It swirled through all the great cities and plains and it brought rainstorms and cold winds. The storm was like an iceberg pushing everything in front of it. Birds, light animals, branches were in the air, banging against and damaging each other.

In Banaras a group of exhausted vultures finally took refuge by a wall. They no longer looked like kings as they thought they did when they perched on carrion. Their feathers faced every direction and they were too ashamed to look at each other. They just lay there, shivering, near a ditch, waiting for something worse to happen.

One morning an old merchant was walking on his way to bathe when he saw these poor creatures. He built them a fire and made them huddle around it. He found some food for them and then he got someone who worked for him to keep an eye on them until they had fully recovered.

A few days later the vultures flew off into the mountains. The first thing they did was organize a meeting and hold counsel. They were all deeply impressed by the merchant from Banaras and they all thought they owed him a favour. But what could they do? The meeting lasted all day and all night. What could they do? Well, a jury or a committee of vultures is like any committee of humans. As someone said, you put five intelligent people together and they vote like an idiot.

The solution the vultures came up with was this.

As the merchant had been going off to bathe, and so was not wearing too much, they assumed he had very few clothes to his name. They didn't even know what his name was. But they did know where he lived, so they decided to cruise in the air above Banaras and whenever they saw a stray garment or piece of clothing they would swoop down, pick it up and fly off to drop it into the merchant's garden.

Soon the city of Banaras seemed to be in the midst of a mad plague of sarong and dhoti stealing birds. No laundry was safe. Mrs. G——

lost several sarees left to dry on the bushes of her front lawn. They were seen travelling in the air carried by five vultures. Eventually they floated down into the merchant's yard along with, on average, forty pieces of clothing a day.

The merchant had no idea what was going on, so he just stored all these objects in his back room. The population, however, was getting furious. They knew it was the vultures—there were too many witnesses. There were complaints to the mayor, then to the priests and then to the King. The vultures were plundering the city. They were even removing caps off people's heads now. The famous actress M——R had her blouse removed as she lay sunning herself on her porch.

The King sent for the best vulture-catcher in the country. But he took a week getting there and by then residents no longer saw any humour in the situation and who could blame them? Nothing could be washed in a public well without disappearing, nothing could be washed in a river or left in a bucket; the actress M——R had left town in embarrassment. Even the flag above the city was ripped from its pole and was carried away in the beak of a vulture.

The vulture catcher set up his secret traps. The method is still a secret so no one can write about how he did it. It was a great secret and his trade was based on it. He didn't like to talk about it. And a few years later it went with him to the grave, still somewhere in that vulture-catching brain of his. He knew everything about vultures. He set his snares and gins everywhere—in the strangest places, places so strange we cannot even talk about them, for all this fell under the Official Secrets Act of Banaras.

Within a day the first vulture was caught and of course it turned out to be the Bodhisattva in his most recent reincarnation. He had been innocently dipping his beak into a tin of condensed milk and then wiping his beak on a newspaper to get the sticky substance off when he was captured by that secret system we cannot write about. Though without words I can draw what it looked like:

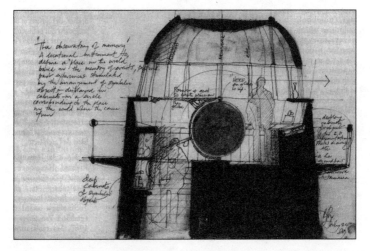

There. Now let's get on.

A huge crowd surrounded the vulture and the vulture catcher as they walked towards the King's palace. The merchant of Banaras had been on his way to see the King on some (secret) business and he recognized the vulture as one of those he had saved. He followed and kept an eye on the situation.

The King was given the vulture to execute. He pulled out his jewelled sword and stood there for a moment. The King in fact at this point was not sure what the ceremony was. Was he supposed to say something? And to whom? So as people do in situations like this he started talking to the vulture as if it was human.

"You! You have been stealing our clothes, our costumes, our veils, sarongs, sarees—"

"Yes sir," said the bird. These two words, of course, surprised everyone.

"Why? And what have you done with all of them?" The King hadn't noticed that he was in conversation with a bird.

"We gave them to the merchant, that one there, because he saved our lives. One good turn deserves another. That's what we decided at our meeting. He saved our lives during the storm. You remember the storm, Your Highness, don't you?"

The King was being charmed by the talking vulture. He couldn't execute a bird that talked. So he sheathed his jewelled sword and got into the spirit of the discussion. "Vultures—they say—can spy a body a mile away." He paused for effect, walking around, nodding to himself wisely. "But you couldn't see the trap waiting for you that was set up by my catcher . . . ."

He was in fact quoting two famous and ridiculously ponderous lines, which went like this:

"A *vulture sees a corpse one hundred leagues away,*
da dum,
When thou alightest on a trap dost thou not see it, pray?"

The vulture replied by spouting out the next two lines of the well-known piece. The vulture squawked:

"*When life is coming to an end, and death's hour draws nigh,*
da dum,
Though you may come up close, no trap or snare you spy."

It used to be a well-known piece then, but now no one knows where it came from. (And no one really knows what this all means, but somehow this story has been passed down for years as a wise bit of repartee. What *does* it mean? Is it a bad translation? Was the real conversation whispered secretly back and forth between the King and the vulture? In any case, everyone has pretended to understand it for 900 years. It could mean something, and probably does. But not that much. Something about death binding us . . . .)

The King at this point felt this should be the closure to the conversation. He had been one-upped by a vulture and he didn't want to drag it out any more. He turned to the merchant and whispered secretly into his ear about what he should do. And at this point I would tell you what he said but it also falls under the Official Secrets Act of Banaras so I cannot repeat it. And anyway, how would I know? Was I a vulture in an earlier life? Was I a king?

THE HOPPER

RETOLD BY RAJ RAMANATHAPILLAI

THERE WERE TWO RABBIT BROTHERS who lived in a beautiful part of the jungle. They were very spirited, energetic and joyful. Their only real fault was that they often became competitive.

One day, in a clearing partially lit by the sun, they were chasing each other, running back and forth happily. They were still running after one another when, in mid stride, they suddenly saw a hunter. He was sitting under a tree eating his lunch of hoppers. He looked content as he continued to lounge there, picking at his food dreamily, until he became increasingly tired and finally fell over into a deep sleep—leaving his leftover hoppers lying there beside him.

The rabbit brothers were so thrilled. They couldn't believe the chance they now had, and they stood completely still, staring at the hoppers. Their mouths began watering for food. They began to creep, very slowly, towards the sleeping hunter, keeping themselves low down in the grass until they were within inches of the hoppers. Then they leaned forward silently and picked up a big hopper. With the food in their grasp, they sprang away in the opposite direction, running crazily into the forest, dodging past leaves and bushes until they couldn't run any farther. When they stopped they could hardly breathe, but they calmed themselves and eventually found a huge tree in whose shade they could sit and enjoy their new food.

The eldest brother held the hopper up to his nose and said:, "*Ah*, what a delicious smell! I'd love just to eat the whole thing."

"No!" said the younger brother. "That's not fair. I want my share."

The big brother replied, "Well, since I am the eldest, I must have the biggest share and you can have the rest of it."

The younger brother quickly responded, "No! That's not right—it should be divided equally!"

"Like this?" The big brother took the hopper and split it into two pieces. "This will be my half."

The younger brother shouted, "Now you're *cheating*. You took the biggest piece!"

He held up his half of the hopper as he said this, waving it in the air in front of his brother's nose, and the two brothers soon started quarrelling and fighting.

From above, in the branches of the huge tree, a clever monkey was watching the rabbit brothers fighting over the hopper. "Wait!" the monkey shouted. "Stop fighting!"

Then, still sitting in the tree, he lectured them:

"Fighting is bad. It will bring violence to the world, and it will also draw out bad things in your nature. There are so many ways that beings can solve their problems without fighting. Since I am older and wiser than you, I will propose a solution."

Both rabbits thought this was good advice, especially since it was offered from someone older and wiser than themselves. Besides, they were hungry and in an extreme hurry to start eating their hopper.

The monkey said, "Look here, brothers, I have a balancing scale. I will take the hopper and put one piece on either side of the balance to make sure both of you get an equal quantity. But if I am to do this favour for you and act as your judge, I will do so under one condition."

"What is the condition?" the brothers asked.

"Well . . . whenever you weigh something on the balance, one side usually weighs more than the other. Therefore, in order to balance your pieces of the hopper, it will be necessary to remove a portion from the side that weighs more. As my fee, I want that portion for myself. Do you both agree to this?"

The rabbit brothers thought the monkey sounded very reasonable and intelligent. So they agreed.

The monkey then brought out his balancing scale and set it up in the shaded branches overhead. He climbed down to the ground, took the two pieces of hopper and climbed back up his tree as the two brothers watched anxiously. The monkey expertly set a piece of hopper on each side of the scale. One piece *did* weigh more than the other. The monkey took a bite out of that piece and calmly replaced it on the scale. Now it appeared the other piece weighed more . . . .

While the rabbit brothers watched helplessly from the shade below the tree, the monkey continued taking bites from one piece and then the other piece, until the whole hopper was gone.

THE DOG WHO DRANK FROM SOCKS

RETOLD BY GRIFFIN ONDAATJE

EARLY IN THE MORNING, miles into the country, Abdul's car broke down and he had to push it to the side of the road. An hour passed and he still couldn't get it started again. He kicked it and decided to leave the useless vehicle behind. He began to walk towards the nearest village. Now, after walking for miles, he was getting tired and very thirsty. He looked through the trees along the road but there were no houses, and as he became more desperate, he became angrier too. His suit stuck to his body and the sun began to burn his neck. He was thirsty when he left the car, and now after miles of walking through this awful countryside where there were no houses and no ponds or streams, the thirst had become too much for him.

"If I do not find some water soon I will die!" he shouted, dramatically.

Some birds flew away from the trees after he had shouted this so loudly. He watched them, envying the way they could fly up over the land and see where water was.

He continued along the road, looking for a well to drink from, but any well he came to was dried out. He began to worry. He searched in the forest along the road, stepping through bushes, and then walked back into the bright sunlight even more thirsty than before. He felt lost. A big burning dryness was in his chest.

But he kept walking. Soon he entered a small field where there was a muddy pool of water. Three water-buffalo were standing in it, drinking. Abdul stopped to look at them. The buffalo stood looking at him too. Long strands of grass hung from their mouths and water dribbled off their chins. Their faces were covered in flies but their eyes had a calm expression—staring at Abdul for several minutes without blinking. Then, they lost interest in him and shook their heads and blinked to get the flies away as they lowered their mouths to the water. Abdul, frustrated, also shook his head, and turned down the road.

At last he came to a field where there was a large well, and when he leaned over to look into it he could hear grains of sand falling into water. He looked around quickly for a rope or a bucket.

There was nothing.

He shouted, close to tears. Exasperated, he took off his new shoes and climbed over the wall and began sliding down, scraping his knees and elbows badly, and when he had slid down ten feet he made a small splash in the water. It was only a few inches deep. Yet the water felt cold on his ankles. He cupped his hands and drank. He drank handfuls of it, then bent down on his hands and knees to drink with his mouth. He drank and drank until his stomach was full and he couldn't drink any more.

Abdul climbed back up out of the well.

When he was about to pick up his shoes, he heard something whining and he looked across the empty yard.

A dog was lying beneath a bush. Its mouth and whiskers were covered in dust, and it lay there as if it was dead. Only its eyes moved.

With a shock Abdul recognized that thirst. It had led him through the hot day to this near-empty well along the road, and had also led this dog here. He saw the suffering, felt by him minutes ago, now in the dog's eyes. Looking at this wretched dog he was amazed to think that only moments earlier he had felt the same way.

It shocked him to feel sympathy for this animal and before he realized what he was doing, he turned and climbed back down the well.

When he got to the bottom he suddenly realized he had nothing to carry water with.

He searched around in the water, thinking he'd maybe find an old coconut shell or something. But there wasn't anything. He could've used his shoes but he was only wearing socks. So he took both his socks off and sank them in the water. He gripped them in his teeth and climbed back out as quickly as he could.

He rushed the leaking socks over to the dog, knelt down and held them open so that the dog could drink. The dog drank dry the two socks and then licked them, rolling them in the dust.

Then the dog licked Abdul's pant cuffs, which were still wet, and Abdul stood back, slightly disgusted, but glad the dog was happy now.

Then, with socks and shoes in hand, Abdul walked to the road with the dog who drank from socks and they headed off in the direction of the nearest village.

NARADA'S LESSON

RETOLD BY P.K. PAGE

NARADA WAS A SERIOUS MAN. A good man. Perhaps a godly man. He attended to his prayers, his work, and his family responsibilities. He even found time for his community. All things considered, he was a happy man. But there was a mystery in his life: one he could neither solve nor forget.

His teachers told him the world was illusion—Maya. His senses told him they were wrong.

Surely the earth beneath his feet was real, and the sky above his head? Was the sun, when it shone, not hot enough to burn him? Did the rain, when it fell, not soak him to the skin? The fragrance of jasmine blossoms, the taste of his wife's curries . . . how could they be illusions? To say nothing of the feel of his children's arms around his neck, and his wife's kisses. *They* were not imagination. Of that he was certain. And yet?

He brooded over his enigma a great deal and finally he raised the subject with his good friend Chandra.

"How is it possible," he asked, "that everything I touch, taste, smell, hear and see is an illusion? That is what my teacher tells me. It is not that I don't believe my teacher. It is just that I *can't* believe him." He kicked a stone and winced at the pain in his toe. Was the pain in his toe not real?

"I see it this way," his friend replied. "We have a movie inside us— our movie—in glorious technicolor with stereo sound. Our eyes are the projector. Everything we see and hear is this movie—everything we think and feel. And because we never leave the cinema, cannot leave the cinema, we believe what we see, and we call it reality. It is, in fact, illusion."

Narada was quiet for a long time. "If what you say is true," he said at last, "then you are part of my illusion. Right?"

"Right!" his friend laughed.

"So what happens to you when you leave my presence? Surely I am not the *cause* of your existence."

"Of course not—don't you see? I have a moving picture, too," Chandra said.

"And they fit neatly together?" Narada asked. "Tell me how." And then, bewildered, "And what about your wife's movie? And your father's and your mother's and . . . and . . . and . . ." He gave up as the complexity of it overwhelmed him.

"Try not to question everything this way," his friend said. "Just accept what our teacher says. Even your questioning is part of Maya. Our illusions are a spell upon us. Your questions are part of that spell."

Narada knew Chandra was right—for Chandra. But Narada was not Chandra. He had to question things. His very nature seemed to insist upon it.

"Perhaps if I pray more, fast more, practise my devotions more rigorously," he thought, "I can learn to question less. And if I question less, perhaps I shall understand." So Narada applied himself with greater dedication.

Narada's children grew up. His wife died. With fewer and fewer worldly pressures upon him he became a model devotee, and spent the better part of his days in meditation and prayer. There were even those who considered him a holy man.

But Narada himself knew that he was not holy, and he was as full of doubts and questions as he had always been.

One day, deep in his usual prayer, he was aware of a sudden light and when he opened his eyes, the god Vishnu stood before him. Blazing, like the sun.

Was *this* Maya? Narada wondered. Was the god, himself, part of his dream? But before he had time to wonder further, the god spoke.

"I have come to grant you a wish."

Narada had only one wish. One prayer. "O great Vishnu, show me the magic power of your Maya."

"Follow me," Vishnu replied, and with an inscutable smile on his beautiful, cruel mouth, he led Narada from his leafy shelter to a blinding desert that flashed like the blades of swords.

It was hotter than anywhere in Narada's experience. Even the god himself seemed parched and exhausted. Shielding their eyes and peering into the light, they saw some vague disturbance in the air that might be a distant village.

"Fetch me water," Vishnu begged.

"Certainly, Lord," Narada answered and he set off towards what, as he moved nearer, looked like a cluster of straw huts. But he was uncertain whether it was village or mirage. He was even uncertain whether he was asleep or awake.

Finally, dehydrated and weary, he came to a small hut. To his great relief, the door was solid beneath his knock. A beautiful girl answered and Narada looked into her eyes. They were the god's eyes.

When she bade him welcome her voice was a silken rope that led him into a house so familiar he felt he had lived there forever. He forgot what he had come for. The family members received him with honour and he lived among them as if he belonged, sharing the burdens and joys of their simple life. Before long, to everyone's delight, he married the beautiful girl.

Twelve years passed. During that time the couple had three children, and Narada assumed his family responsibilities with diligence and love. When his father-in-law died, Narada became head of the household—managing the estate, tending the cattle and cultivating the fields.

In the twelfth year, the rainy season began with torrential rains. Day after day storm clouds gathered and deluged the plain below. Day after day the despairing villagers tried to patch their leaking roofs and, fearful for their cattle, drove them to the higher land where they herded them into a makeshift corral.

"It must ease up soon," the villagers told each other. But it did not.

Days turned to weeks and still the rains continued. The people became accustomed to being wet, grew used to the many sounds of water—dripping, oozing, running, rushing. Small streams overflowed their banks and turned into rivers. The surrounding fields became first a bog, then a vast, shallow lake whose rising water demolished the makeshift corrals and carried away the pitifully lowing cattle.

With what few possessions they could pack, the desperate villagers struggled to escape. Supporting his wife with one hand, leading the two children with the other, and carrying the baby on his back, Narada set his face to the driving rain. Darkness fell. It was treacherous underfoot and the current pulled the children along faster than they could walk. Narada stumbled and the child slipped from his back. In an attempt to save her he let go of the other two and all three were swept away. Before he had regained his own footing his wife's hand was wrenched from his and she too disappeared into the night. If she cried out, he did not hear her above the roaring of the wind and the waters.

Exhausted, and with nothing left to lose, Narada had neither the heart nor the strength to struggle. Knocked off balance and half drowned, his near-lifeless body—now mere flotsam—was borne along by the rushing current and thrown at the foot of a cliff. When Narada regained consciousness he saw a sheet of filthy water. In it the straw huts from his village bobbed and swirled, inconsequential as wasps' nests. Narada wept.

"Child!" The familiar voice nearly stopped his heart. "Where is the water you went to fetch for me? I have waited over half an hour."

Narada opened his eyes. The glittering, sun-drenched desert stretched all around him. Vishnu the god was at his shoulder.

"Child," the god spoke again, the same enigmatic smile on his beautiful, cruel lips, "*now* do you understand the secret of my Maya?"

POWER MISUSED

RETOLD BY S. SAMARASINGHE

A CERTAIN VILLAGE HEADMAN, or Gamarala, had implicit faith in the Goddess Ritta who was believed to confer blessings on anyone who prayed to her. The headman's forefathers, too, had had faith in the Goddess Ritta. As a boy this villager therefore used to utter the short incantation *May Goddess Ritta bless me* whenever he began work or set out from home.

One morning, late in his life as a married man, he had to leave home and go to a distant village. As he set out, he took the first step with his right leg (an auspicious way to start a journey) and he uttered the phrase *May Goddess Ritta bless me*. He walked for several miles and then rested at an ambalama, a rest-house where anyone could stop and sit. No one was there at the time and he entered the building. He waited for a while and walked a few steps away to drink water from a spout. When he turned to go back in he saw a beautiful woman in a sari standing in front of him. The Gamarala was astonished and pleased to see her. He could not believe his eyes.

The lady came forward in a graceful, effortless sort of way, and spoke out to him: "Why do you utter the words *May Goddess Ritta bless me* whenever you start some work or set out on a journey?"

He was nervous, but he answered immediately: "I have implicit faith in the Goddess."

"Well," she said, "I am the Goddess Ritta. What do you want? I will endow you today with a boon of your choice. You have only to say what you want."

"I won't do anything without asking my wife. Could I have your permission to run home, see what she says and then come back?"

The Goddess granted him permission and the Gamarala ran home to find his wife, but when he saw her she was crying and in a terrible rage. Their neighbour, Babanis the farmer, had allowed his black bull loose again and it had upturned all the plantain trees that grew in their field.

The Gamarala was too excited to console his wife and he quickly told her of his meeting with the Goddess Ritta and the blessing she was willing to bestow upon him. He told his wife to imagine the fruits of such a blessing: having *anything* one wishes.

But the Gamarala's wife was in such a state of anger that she didn't listen. She shouted, in despair, that she didn't want any blessings other than the power to punish the bull and have revenge for her plantain trees.

The excited Gamarala took his wife's words literally, and he ran off to see the Goddess. He ran up to her, out of breath.

"I would like to have the power to destroy!" he said.

Without hesitation the Goddess granted this request, and disappeared.

The Gamarala stared around himself breathlessly, somewhat exhilarated. He peered into the trees above to see if the Goddess was somewhere near by still watching him. Even though he saw no one, he slowly sensed he wasn't quite alone. A strange feeling of power seemed to be with him now. The feeling grew quite suddenly and for a moment he felt afraid, but then he thought how lucky he was to possess such a gift.

The Gamarala stood alone in the road, growing more certain of his good fortune, and then he turned and ran back home in a hurry—forgetting about his original journey completely.

Late that night, the Gamarala and his wife were woken up by strange noises outside their window. The neighbour's bull had come back to feed upon all the plantain bushes it had pulled down earlier.

The Gamarala ran out into his yard, half asleep, and shouted at the bull. The bull took no notice of him and kept on eating. But the Gamarala was wide awake now and recalled his new power—he decided to use this power, and so he shouted out again to the bull, saying, *May you be destroyed!* The bull fell to the ground and died.

Babanis, the next-door neighbour, came running towards the Gamarala's house. He had heard the shouting and had jumped out of bed and run over to stop his bull from causing further damage. When he entered the yard now, though, he saw his bull lying dead on the grass and the Gamarala standing proudly beside it.

"What have you done?" he asked, as he walked up slowly to the Gamarala in total disbelief.

"I have the power to destroy anything," the Gamarala answered excitedly, clenching his fists.

Babanis looked at the dead bull again and then held his head and started shouting and crying, telling the Gamarala that he was cruel and heartless.

The Gamarala, angry and confident of his new power, said nothing to his neighbour at first, and then decided to reveal his strength again and shouted, *May you be destroyed also!* Babanis suddenly fell to the ground and died.

The dead man's family ran out to fight the Gamarala, but as soon as they came into the yard he shouted his curse at them also, and they fell forward and died in front of him.

The Gamarala's wife ran out of the house and was horrified to see all that had happened. She screamed at her husband and ran up to try to stop him. She gripped his arm and tried to pull him back but he turned immediately and shouted the curse.

She fell down and died beside him.

He had slipped and fallen to the ground too—but he quickly got to his feet again.

There was no one around him left alive, but as the power continued to flow inside him, he shouted the curse once more, and in the next instant he fell down dead.

THE UNICORN AND THE
GRAPEVINE

TIMOTHY FINDLEY

. . . THE BODHISATTVA, LIFE-TRAVELLER *on the way to becoming Buddha, was once an antelope . . . speaking in human language that had been perfected in the course of a hundred incarnations. The colouring of this antelope was as bright as pure gold, and with the soft gemlike lustre of his horns and hoofs, he was of surpassing beauty. Knowing how slight humanity's compunction was, he preferred to stay in the depths of the forest, avoiding human contact.*

Thus it is written concerning one of the many incarnations of Buddha; and thus can we call to mind another creature of great beauty who once lived in the wilds, far from humankind. This was a magical creature of wisdom and of gentle powers—including the power of human speech: the Unicorn.

Many have lamented the passing of this wondrous and unique beast. One new-day writer, in telling the story of the universal Flood, related how the Unicorn—that flower-fed marvel of the forest—perished on board the Great Ark, a victim of human brutality. As has been said before, and as can still be said, to our dismay: cruelty is nothing more than a failure of the imagination. It was the extinction of the Unicorn, our new-day writer explains, that caused all the magic to fade from the world.

Sadly, I must confess: that new-day writer is your present storyteller. But wonders never cease, and I can tell you now that your storyteller no longer holds to new-day ways. You will see the truth of this when I reveal to you what has since been discovered regarding the fate of the Unicorn, and the magic it carried onto the earth.

This splendid beast, whose powers so exceeded its delicate dimensions, first came into being within that same Supreme Imagination that created us all, and that created, too, the magnificent world in which we all live. When time was ripe for its birth, the Unicorn stepped out of the Supreme Imagination into the sun-dappled seclusion of the forest, and thus, into the experience—and the greedy grasp—of humankind.

In time, as other storytellers have noted, the Unicorn eluded our grasp and abandoned its forest home. But not through death. Not through extinction. The Supreme Imagination does not embrace and will not tolerate extinction. Instead of disappearance, it decrees transformation: not obliteration, but the evolution of one being into another. (If you search the word another, you will find the word one, itself transformed.) This way, the Unicorn retreated into the safety of the human imagination—where anyone can catch a glimpse of its beauty, whether in paintings or in paragraphs. Wherever the human imagination thrives, the Unicorn lives. When human imagination fails, as has been said—it dies.

It is not just the Unicorn born of the Supreme Imagination that lives in this inner realm. It is every unicorn that ever stepped upon the earth. Let me tell you of one of them.

There was once a unicorn whose name was "Half-wit," because his head was adorned with but a single horn. He suffered dreadfully from ridicule. Other hoofed creatures proudly displayed a pair of horns—horns being the outward sign of wit and wisdom.

One day, angry and hurt, Half-wit resolved to take action against his disfigurement. He chose a place in the forest where a rocky outcropping thrust a hard, sharp edge of obsidian out towards the trees. Measuring carefully with his eye, the unicorn lowered his head and charged at the rock, hoping it would split his horn in two, and thus provide him with an acceptable appearance. Unhappily, he misjudged his aim, and the tip of his horn, deflected by the bright obsidian, buried itself solidly in an adjacent cleft. And there it stuck, despite his frantic efforts to free himself from the rock's unyielding grasp.

The other animals gathered to laugh at the unicorn's plight. "Half-wit! Half-wit!" they cried. "He will soon have no wits at all!" He suffered their cruel humour in silence until—looking down—he saw what was happening near his blue-veined hooves. There, the shoot of a budding grapevine had begun to grow up the rock towards the unicorn's head. It was the kind of grapevine along which news is able to pass. The voice of this particular vine reached out towards the ears of the animal assemblage:

"Tell me, you who scorn another's adversity, what is the most magnificent thing you have ever seen?"

"The sun!" cried a voice.

"And why," said the grapevine, "do you call the sun magnificent?"

"Because," the voice said, "although it leaves us at the end of every day, it never fails to light both the business and the pleasure of our lives."

"I see," mused the grapevine, sprouting three new leaves and two new tendrils even as it spoke. "And what, may I ask, is wonderful?"

"The moon!" another voice called out. And then, in response to the grapevine's query: "because it looks down at us with a changing face that signals how time is passing . . . ."

"Indeed," said the grapevine, waving its leaves and flourishing its purple fruit. "And what, pray tell, is inspiring?"

A third voice was heard: "The stars are inspiring," and, without waiting for the question, "because their patterns in the sky draw pictures that tell us the stories of our beginnings . . . ."

The grapevine grew in silence for a moment, and then sent its words once more towards the circle of animals. "Does everything magnificent, wonderful and inspiring reside in the sky?" it asked—itself straining upwards. "Do you mean you look around you and find nothing here to marvel at on earth?"

As the animals shuffled their hooves and shifted their eyes, the grapevine continued: "Look, then, at what is growing in this very rock that holds the unicorn so tightly in its grasp. Do you not see? Here is the gold magnificence of the sunflower, reaching up and out towards the blazing orb from which it takes its name; and the white of the wondrous moonflower, opening its petals only at night, beneath the light of its namesake—and the inspirational blue of the starflowers, hanging in their own intriguing patterns from their stems."

The grapevine twisted back towards the unicorn, rustling its words in the direction of the rock's prisoner. "Feed, I charge you, on these earthly wonders, unicorn—and let them free you from your present predicament."

The unicorn turned his head as far as he could, and, reaching out with lips and tongue, tasted of the triad—sunflower, moonflower and starflower. All at once, his eyes widened, and, to the amazement of all who watched, he withdrew his horn from the rock—as one might draw a silver sword from its sheath. At last, he was able to stand erect once more.

Many of the animals—even those who once had laughed at the unicorn—stamped their hooves in approval. Others leapt to the branches around them and sang out their happiness in a song that echoed through the whole wide forest. After all, there is nothing that lives that does not celebrate freedom.

"Tell me, grapevine," the unicorn said at last, when the stamping and the singing had ceased, "what can I do to repay you for setting me free?"

"You can teach all unicorns to live on a diet of flowers," said the grapevine, "from now until the end of time. Thus will the eyes of the unicorn remain wide open to all that is magnificent, wonderful and inspiring here on earth. And from the flowers themselves will come a truly magical power—the power to conquer space and time."

"To conquer space and time!" The unicorn pranced with excitement, while the other animals muttered their envy. "But still, I ask," said the unicorn, "what must I do to merit such wondrous power?"

"Why," said the grapevine, in a quiet voice, "you must spread the word of all the wonders you encounter in your days on earth. You must tell every being that breathes—all the animals and all the people—about the marvels of the place you share."

The unicorn stopped prancing, and thought about this. "All the animals?" he asked. "And all the people?" He frowned at the grapevine. "But how can I possibly go everywhere? And how will I ever have time to speak to everyone?"

The grapevine had become quite weary with its growing and its freeing of the unicorn and now its words could hardly be heard. "Did I not tell you that unicorns would conquer space and time?"

"Yes," said the unicorn, "but how?"

No more words came from the grapevine. It had curled around the rock, and now it was entirely still and silent.

The spectacle of its growth and the wonder of its wisdom seemed to have concluded and the animals began to drift away. For his part, the unicorn, held prisoner for so long, realized how thirsty he was, and he went in search of water. He knew he must be careful where he drank, since many of the pools in various parts of the forest were poisonous. He would have to smell the scent and try the texture and taste the edges of every pool before he could drink.

At last he found a pond he knew to be safe and, having drunk, he decided to leave a mark that would speak the message for others: here you may drink your fill.

And so he scraped with his sharp white hooves at the pond's rocky border and, having left his message, moved on.

This was how he fulfilled his part of the bargain made with the grapevine. Wherever the unicorn went, he left his distinctive marks that advertised the wonders of what he found—the pure, sweet springs of water, the most tender shoots of bamboo, the thickest patches of berries. And once we had learned to read his messages, just as the grapevine had predicted, his words conquered space and time because they could be read no matter how many miles or days the unicorn had travelled since creating them.

How, then, can anyone say that magic has faded from the world? How can you say it, with evidence to the contrary right before your eyes? Are my words not speaking to you now, though miles and years now lie between us? And if there is still such potent magic as that—who knows?—there may still be a unicorn in some wild forest yet to be imagined. A forest of sunflowers, perhaps. Or a field of moonflowers and starflowers gazing up towards their namesakes. But of course, his existence is entirely up to you, since, after all, it is your imagination—if you have one—that must invent him.

KUNDALINI

RETOLD BY CHITRA FERNANDO

LONG AGO, A YOUNG MAN called Muttu lived in Piniwela in Lord Leuke's land. Muttu worked harder than all the other villagers because he was the tallest and the strongest of them all. He rose at dawn, dug, hoed and weeded till the sun was up. Then, he went from village to village, painting new pictures in the temples or repainting old ones. In the evening, he bathed at the village tank beside the paddy fields, washing off the dirt and dust of the day's work. Flocks of birds flew over the fields to their nests: parrots, paddy-birds, herons and cranes. Muttu liked the cranes best, especially as they flew across the sky—legs thrust back, wings spread out, necks outstretched, uttering sad cries.

One evening, happening to look up, Muttu noticed a crane bigger than all the others, flying very low. Its white feathers shone like silver, its golden eyes flashed like jewels. Muttu ran towards it, it was so beautiful. But he didn't run far. The village girls came, laughing and chattering, to fill their water pots at the tank.

"Ah, there you are, Muttu! Your mother is waiting for you. She said she couldn't cook because there's no one to husk coconuts."

"She said you'd left home more than an hour ago."

"You're very clean. Your skin has a golden glow!"

Their playful chatter drowned the ever fainter cries of the cranes. As Muttu walked back with his friends, they chattered about Syma's bull lost again in the forest, about quarrelling Kota and Dhiga, about Rathi and Bindu . . . But here was Dinga waiting for her son.

"Husk the coconuts quickly," she said.

The silver crane with the golden eyes was there again the next day. And the next and the next. One day it came so close, Muttu touched its soft, shiny feathers as it looked at him trustingly with its clear, golden eyes. Suddenly, it rose into the air, turning its long, slender neck, and looking back as Muttu followed.

The crane flew into the forest. Muttu followed, pushing aside creepers and bushes. All at once, he was in a clearing. He looked around. The crane had vanished and before him stood a silvery-haired, golden-eyed woman with a golden skin, the colour of wild honey. Muttu stared at her in wonder and fear.

"No ordinary person can change from a crane into a woman. Who are you? A goddess?"

"No, I'm not a goddess, Muttu. For over a thousand years, men of my race haven't spoken to men of yours."

"What is your race? Who are you?"

"I am Kundalini, daughter of Tilopa. We are people who lived in Lanka before your ancestors came across the sea, tall men in strong ships. Their prince, Vijaya, married Kuveni, our queen. But after a time, he left her. Your people tilled the land, built great tanks, temples and palaces. We have lived hidden away in the forests."

"I know the story of Vijaya and Kuveni. She was an enchantress, a *rakshasini*."

Kundalini shook her head. "We can turn others and ourselves into any form—animal, bird or fish. But we aren't demons. We eat only wild fruit and honey. We own nothing. Is this the way of *rakshasas*?"

"No," said Muttu, "that's not the way of *rakshasas*."

"We are the children of the forest. The leopards are our brothers, the deer are our sisters."

It was getting dark. "I must go home now," said Muttu.

"Tell no one about me."

"That I'll never do. I swear it."

"And where have you been today?" scolded Dinga. "You weren't at the tank. Chop this wood, husk these coconuts. And did you remember the ghee?"

Muttu thought of Kundalini day and night. He felt he couldn't live without her. After his work in the temples, he went straight to the forest clearing. And Kundalini was always there, waiting for him. They bathed in the forest pools, picked the forest flowers, wove them into garlands for each other and walked along the forest paths hand in hand, talking or singing. Kundalini showed Muttu where the sweetest wild honey and the ripest fruits were. And so the days passed.

One evening, Muttu was a long time in the forest. Dinga was angry and frightened. "Why do you go into the forest every day? Your father went often into the forest and one day he never came home again."

Dinga wiped her eyes. Syma, their neighbour, came in.

"Ah, so Muttu is back? I was looking for my bull when I saw you coming out of the forest. What were you doing there, eh, Muttu?"

"Since you make my business yours, Syma, looking for wild honey." He undid the bundle in his hand and took out a honeycomb.

"This is for you, Amme."

"Show me where to find wild honey too," said Syma, as he left.

After that, Syma watched Muttu closely. He even noticed the strange crane by the tank one day.

"Look at the strange crane," he called out to Kota. And as the crane flew quickly away, he threw a stone at it.

One evening, when Muttu returned from the forest, he saw a crowd in front of his house. Syma was talking to them, Dinga was crying. When they saw him, Syma stopped talking. Dinga cried louder.

"What's the matter?" asked Muttu. "What's wrong?"

"He asks what's wrong?" said Syma laughing wildly. "He meets a *rakshasini* who changes from a crane to a woman and he asks what's wrong? Pretending to look for honey and walking around with a *rakshasini* in the forest!"

"We must have a big *thovila* and break the evil spirit's power over him. The forest *rakshasinis* ate up his father but I won't let them eat up my Muttu." Dinga began to cry and beat her breast.

"Lock him up till after the *thovila*. We'll wait for that crane by the tank and kill her," shouted Syma.

Two men dragged Muttu to the headman's house and locked him up in a room at the back. They wanted to kill Kundalini! And he could nothing! He rushed at the door like a maddened bull. But the door was strong; he couldn't break it down. At last, tired out, he fell into a deep sleep. A sudden noise awoke him. He sat up. "Who is there?" he called.

"It's I—I—Kundalini. The cranes told me some men dragged you here. So I changed into a rat-snake and came through a hole in the roof to help you escape."

"But how can we escape?"

"I'll change you into a rat-snake too and we'll escape through the hole in the roof."

A few minutes later, two rat-snakes came out of the hole in the headman's roof, slithered down the outer wall and disappeared into the trees and bushes by the side of the road. Long before dawn, Muttu and Kundalini, humans again, slipped out of Piniwela. They walked a long way till they came to a cart-road running alongside the forest. Coming towards them was a band of happy people, talking, laughing and singing. They were pilgrims returning from Sri Pada. "Karunavai! Karunavai!" they called out when they saw Muttu and Kundalini. "Where are you going to, you two? This is a lonely road."

"We are looking for Diyagala," replied Muttu without thinking.

"Diyagala! That's our village. Do you know anyone in Diyagala?"

"No. My sister and I are looking for work. Times are bad in our village."

"Well, then, come with us. Soon it'll be harvest-time. We'll need extra helpers," said a woman who looked as black and oily as a ball of *kaludodol*. So Muttu and Kundalini went with the oily, black woman who was called Kaluhamy. She invited them to stay with her and asked a hundred and one questions as they walked: In Piniwela how many sacks of rice did they get each harvest? Did the *jak* trees bear well? Were the Piniwela men strong? And the women beautiful? Why did Muttu's sister have those strange eyes? Did many Piniwela women have eyes like that?

Muttu was glad when they reached Diyagala. Some children playing near a clump of mango trees saw them.

"They have returned. The pilgrims have returned from Sri Pada." And they ran through the village, shouting out the news.

"Who are these two?" asked Kaluappu when he saw his wife.

"We'll need more workers at harvest-time. These two are looking for work. They are from Piniwela. Times are bad there they say."

"Hm." Kaluappu looked at them. "You look strong. If you work hard, I'll give you two pieces of silver. If you're lazy, I'll drive you out."

Kaluhamy took them into the kitchen. The hearth was full of ash, the *chatty* pots were black and greasy.

"Light the fire," said Kaluhamy to Muttu.

"And you, first wash these pots, then scrape the coconut. Why do you have your head always covered with that cloth? We're out of the hot sun now. Take it off." Kaluhamy pulled the cloth away. "What strange hair!"

"It's the blessing of the gods," said Muttu quickly. "When we were little children, our mother took us to the Alutnuwara *devale*. Kundalini's hair and eyes changed colour in the Vishnu *devale*. It was a gift from the blue god."

"She's different and I don't like people who are different. I like everybody to be dark and plump like me."

The days passed. Muttu worked with Kaluappu while Kaluhamy shouted orders to Kundalini all day: "Pound the chillies, I want more water from the well. Husk those coconuts. Bring those bags of rice inside. You're not a princess because of your golden eyes and silvery hair. You must work."

And work Kundalini did from morning till night. But she was given only scraps to eat: the rice stuck to the bottom of the pot, the uneaten vegetables on Kaluhamy's plate. Her golden eyes grew less bright, her hair lost its silvery gleam.

"After the harvest, Kaluappu will give us our two pieces of silver. We'll be rich. Then we'll leave," Muttu told her, saddened by the change in her appearance.

When the last sack of rice had been put away, the Diyagala villagers held a great harvest feast. Kundalini sat with the other women, the most beautiful of them all with her golden eyes and silver hair. Muttu asked her to sing and she sang in her sweet, clear voice:

"Can the moon drive the hare away?
Can the sun ever drive the parrot away?
Can the flower ever drive the bee away?
Can you, beloved, drive my grief away?
The moon and the hare together go away.
The sun and the parrot together fly away.
The flower and the bee together flee away.

I cleave to you and my life ebbs away.
With no word to the moon, the hare stole away,
With no word to the sun, the parrot stole away,
With no word to the flower, the bee stole away,
With no word to me, beloved, you stole away.
In the sky the golden stars are vanishing,
In your face the beauty spots are fading,
In the deep fathomless pools the water is drying,
In aeons of sorrow the world is turning, turning."

Kaluhamy listened to Kundalini, her face full of envy and anger. That night she told Kaluappu, "These two can't leave tomorrow. There are other things they must do."

So, the next morning Kaluapu said, "You haven't done enough. There are other things you must do."

"What other things must we do?" asked Muttu.

"You, Muttu, pound these three sacks of rice."

"And what must I do?" asked Kundalini.

"I will tell you, my girl," replied Kaluhamy with an evil smile. "Long ago, I dropped my brass pot into the vila in the forest. Bring it to me or I'll drive a nail into your head."

Kundalini went into the forest and, turning herself into a large fish, she swam to the bottom of the vila. When she came up with her pot, she saw Kaluhamy and several men with sticks and stones waiting for her. Kaluappu and another man were holding Muttu.

"There is the *rakshasini*!" shouted Kaluhamy.

"Kill the demons!" shouted Kaluappu.

In a trice, Kundalini changed Muttu and herself into hawks. The villagers' cries of fear and anger grew fainter and fainter as they flew swiftly to a distant part of the forest. For a while they lived there and were happy. Then, one day Muttu said, "We can't live in this forest forever, Kundalini. I want to paint, to plant things and to watch them grow. I can't live like the wild animals doing nothing. Let's look for a quiet village and live there."

Kundalini sighed and looked longingly at the forest but she said, "We'll go, if you want to, Muttu."

So they left the forest and walked along a cart-road till they came to the highway. After walking many miles, they came at nightfall to a large town. Kundalini was afraid of the people around her so they spent the night in a wide open space just outside the town. They were awoken by the caw-caw of crows and the chatter of mynahs. There were other sounds too: the snorting of bulls, bells jingling, people shouting to each other. They were in a fairground.

"Let's go, Muttu, let's go."

"No one will hurt you, Kundalini. We can earn money here so we must stay."

"All right, we'll stay then," said Kundalini but she wasn't happy.

"Only for a little while, then we'll go."

They were drinking some hot rice *congee* when a small, wiry man with sly eyes came up. Though they hadn't noticed, he'd been looking at Kundalini and Muttu for some time.

"What are you doing at the fair? Where is your stall?" he asked Muttu.

"I have no stall. I have nothing to sell."

"Well, hm, if that's so, well, you see, I am an actor. My name is Hari. Today we are playing Vijaya and Kuveni. I always play Vijaya and my brother, Pani, plays Kuveni. But he is ill. So I was thinking, hm . . . ." He looked at Kundalini.

"You want my sister to act in your play?"

"Yes," said Hari. "I'll pay you well."

Kundalini shook her head vigorously but Muttu took no notice. He said, "All right. She can be Kuveni but I must play Vijaya."

"No. I am Vijaya. That's my part."

"Kundalini can be Kuveni, only if I can be Vijaya. You be the Pote Gura."

Hari frowned but gave in. "All right, you be Vijaya then. I'll tell you both what to do. My things and the other two actors are over there." He pointed to a wooden stage. They walked across.

"I have found Kuveni," said Hari to the two actors. "She'll be Kuveni and . . ." Hari spoke with difficulty ". . . he'll be Vijaya."

By twelve o'clock a large crowd had gathered in front of the stage. The Pote Gura stepped forward.

"Like Indra on earth, Sinhaba ruled Sinhapura.
His fame in its shining light
Was like the sun at noonday's height;
And so was his son's, Prince Vijaya's fame,
Yes, it was as lovely and as bright."

"Now the noble prince Vijaya with seven hundred warriors sailed from Dambadiva and in Lanka he met the rakshasini, Kuveni."

The curtains parted. Kundalini was sitting on the stage. In her hand was a spindle and she was weaving. The crowd looked at her strange beauty in silence. Some shouted excitedly:

"She is Kuveni! Watch her carefully. See she does no evil."

"Where is Prince Vijaya? Where is our Prince?" shouted others.

"Silence!" ordered the Pote Gura. "Prince Vijaya will appear at the right time. Listen:

"Seated in the nuga shade
Where soft flower-scented breezes played
A lovely rosey garland she displayed
Her tender rounded arm,
As she her golden spindle plied.
Her nail-tips long are as the tips of parrots' bills
A half-smile on her lips as narrow-eyed
Her glinting glance belied
The secret wish to kill."

But Kuveni didn't kill Vijaya. They lived together for many years till Vijaya, tiring of Kuveni, left her. And sorrowfully she wanders through the great forest of Lanka:

"Soft breezes and waters cool she learns
Are as to her as fire that burns
Petals soft pierce her like sharpest thorns,
The koil's notes, the cuckoo's call like iron spears
Leave her hearing racked and torn.
How can this parting grief be borne?"

The Pote Gura finished. The people clapped, shouted, laughed and cried. "Again! We want the story of Kuveni and Vijaya again." Muttu and Kundalini played the story of Vijaya and Kuveni thrice that day. In the evening, they were all so tired, they were ready to drop. But Hari was pleased.

"We have earned a lot of money today. We're now rich." He turned to Muttu. "You . . . you go to the roti stall. Here is money. Bring us roti, sambol, meat, fish—everything."

Muttu took the money and ran across. He didn't like taking orders from Hari but he was hungry.

Hari turned to Kundalini. "Tomorrow I will play Vijaya. Much better than Muttu. Live with me. Be my wife. We will be rich, very rich."

"After we eat, Muttu and I are going to leave. We don't want to stay in this town."

"So you don't like me, ah? You want to go. Rakshasini! Go then, go!"

Muttu came up with the food.

"And don't eat my food, don't eat it. Go, go! Rakshasini, go!"

Hearing Hari's angry voice, the other two actors came up.

"This woman is a rakshasini, a kuveni. Kill her!"

"We think so too. Look at her strange hair and eyes. She's a rakshasini. Kill her!"

"I am Prince Vijaya," said Muttu. "I'll kill all three of you, if you touch Kundalini." Clenching his fists, he stepped forward but he saw three dogs instead of three angry men. Howling mournfully, they ran into town with their tails between their legs.

"I turned Hari and his friends into dogs. I was afraid they'd kill you. They will turn into men again tomorrow. Let's go now—quickly!"

"We can't live among people, I can see that now," said Muttu. "We'll live in the forest but close to the village. We'll walk along the highway till we come to a cart-road. That'll take us to the forest."

After walking for many hours, they came at last to the edge of a great forest. They were tired and hungry. Seeing a bunch of ripe, juicy mangoes on the highest branch of a mango tree, Muttu said, "I'll climb up and get those mangoes."

"No," said Kundalini, "it's easier for me to get them." Turning into a monkey, she ran up the tree, picked the mangoes, then turned into a woman again. But someone was watching her—a young boy with a squint eye. Muttu smiled and offered him a mango but he spat at Kundalini and ran away.

"Let's leave," begged Kundalini. "Let's leave."

"I'll eat just one mango. Then we'll go." Muttu began to peel a mango but before he could eat it they heard footsteps, voices.

The squint-eyed boy appeared again. "There she is, there is the rak-shasini," he shouted. Several men ran forward with burning torches in their hands, which they threw at Kundalini. Kundalini and Muttu ran like the wind, two swift-footed deer, deep into the forest and came out on the other side where they took their own forms again. The sun was setting. They heard the chatter of parrots, the calls of woodpeckers and the sad cries of the cranes flying to their nests. They heard the song of the carter going home to his evening meal.

"There's a village close by," said Kundalini

"Yes," replied Muttu.

They looked at each other.

"I must go, Muttu, back to my people and you must go back to yours. I long for the silence of the forest, for my brother, the leopard, and my sister, the deer. Life with your people has brought me only sor-row. But you will be rewarded for your kindness to me. One day you will be a famous painter. Lord Leuke himself will send for you."

Muttu couldn't speak. Tears ran down his cheeks and he covered his face with his hands. When he uncovered it, he was alone. For days he wandered down the forest paths, not caring where he went. One day, unknowingly, he took a path leading out of the forest. Weak and faint, he stumbled and fell. Close to this place was a temple. Some monks returning from an alms-giving saw him lying on the road and carried him inside. They gave him hot rice congee and looked after him till he was strong again. Then the chief monk sent for him.

"Where do you come from?"

"From Piniwela on the other side of the forest."

"But that's more than a hundred miles away. What are you doing here?"

Muttu didn't answer.

"You don't wish to answer. Never mind. What can you do? What's your trade?"

"I am a temple painter."

The chief monk smiled happily. "Our temple walls need to be repainted. Will you repaint our temple walls?"

"Gladly," said Muttu.

So Muttu began to work. On the first wall he painted the Mahasuka Jataka, on the second the Hamsa Jataka, on the third the Kokalika Jataka and on the fourth wall he painted the story of Kundalini. All four walls, now covered with new pictures, glowed like colourful tapestries. The monks looked at the walls and were pleased with three of them. They were not pleased with the fourth.

"What is this story? This isn't a Jataka story," they told Muttu. "Why did you paint this story on our temple wall? We must tell the chief monk about it."

The chief monk came and looked at all four walls. Then he said, "The story of Kundalini isn't a Jataka story, but like them it teaches us the wisdom of the Dhamma. We must be compassionate to all living beings even though they are different from us. Let the story of Kundalini remain."

All the villagers came to see the new paintings. Never before had they seen such life-like people, birds and animals, such delicate flowers, such glowing trees! The fame of the painting spread throughout the land. One day Lord Leuke himself came to see them.

"Come and paint for me," he said to Muttu. "I am building a great new temple. Be my master-painter." Many great lords wanted Muttu to paint for them. He did not paint the story of Kundalini again but she appeared, nevertheless, in all his paintings in one form or another.

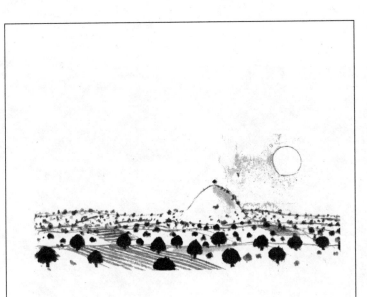

SCARLESS FACE

RETOLD BY GRIFFIN ONDAATJE

SCARLESS FACE WAS A LUCKY and blessed elephant. Though he didn't know it, he was protected from all of the world's pain, ugliness and cruelty because he was favoured by the King. He had never suffered the slightest hardship; nor did he know that hardship existed, since he had never in all of his life gone for a walk outside the palace. He had glimpsed the city through the palace gates once—and what he saw looked quite pleasant. Sometimes he heard voices and songs over the palace wall, and they were pleasant too. People threw flowers over this wall, or fresh sugar cane, which Scarless Face strolled over and ate. Children came to visit him in small groups and gave him handfuls of rice. Now in old age, Scarless Face had grown very comfortable in his roomy stall in the royal elephant stables, right below the King's window. He never suffered from the slightest fear or hunger. He never had a stomach ache or a bad dream. He was relaxed and lived like a young prince, and he was always funny and happy and everyone liked him and thought he was peaceful and wise. But one day his luck ran out— as it often can. Scarless Face didn't wander outside the palace and discover the world's pain, ugliness or cruelty. He didn't have to, since, one night, it all found him. It crept into the royal elephant stables and sat just outside his stall.

It wasn't really pain, ugliness or cruelty that had come to him, just three thieves who had managed to sneak over the walls. By chance, they gathered outside his stall to make plans for a robbery.

The thieves weren't interested in Scarless Face, and didn't even look in his direction. But Scarless Face had never seen a thief before, and had never heard people using such harsh language. His huge ears noticed a tone in their voices that suggested they were—unhappy. Mean perhaps. The words the men used were strange. They talked about shocking things. Scarless Face stopped chewing the coconut he was eating and stood still and listened as new swear words and violent stories came his way.

After listening, Scarless Face began to feel dizzy. His stomach tensed up and his heart pounded in his chest.

He decided to look out of his stall—and so he leaned forward slightly and, without turning his head, glanced both ways—one small eye on either side of his face staring into the dark. He hoped to catch sight of a guard, a sweeper—anyone. But he saw only the dark outline of these three men. There was no one else around.

Scarless Face stepped back into his stall and listened some more . . . .

"We've got to do it right this time," one of the thieves said, ". . . no fooling around. I'll club the two guards while you guys kick them. We'll tie them up and take the key. Then we'll break into the . . ."

Scarless Face was worried. He felt helpless. This helplessness began to overcome him and he didn't know what to do, and even as he tried to calm himself down it was as if the happiness he had always known had been taken away, suddenly, like a bowl of food. The world outside looked bare and empty, and for the first time in his life fear crept through him. He'd lived peacefully all these years, but now he was alone in the middle of the night as these strange men continued to swear and scheme right in front of him. They talked about climbing up through the King's *window!*

The fear and confusion Scarless Face felt made his eyes water and he stood there motionless.

"So," the thief continued, "when we've got the silver we'll throw the torches on the floor and climb out this way."

The thieves talked late into the night and disappeared just before dawn. But they came back the next night, and the next, discussing ways to climb walls, and fight and steal.

And all the while Scarless Face listened he was growing more and more confused and distressed. He thought these men were sent to teach him to become mean and violent too. And being an innocent and impressionable old elephant, Scarless Face gradually came to feel that his world was falling apart. He grew convinced that cruelty and violence were all there was—just as he had been convinced before he met these thieves that kindness and joy were all that existed.

On the third night, Scarless Face stood still, waving his ears and staring into space.

By sunrise, gold light had spread over everything, but as far as Scarless Face could see all goodness had vanished from the world. So that morning, when an elephant-keeper arrived in front of Scarless Face's stall and placed two buckets of water at his feet, he was shocked to find himself lifted high up into the air and thrown powerfully to the ground. He opened his eyes just in time to see Scarless Face's foot about to step on him, but he managed to roll away to safety. Scarless Face turned to a second mahout who came running up and tossed him into the air, and a third man, and then, in a fury, he tore up any bushes and plants standing near by.

Scarless Face's outburst was so unexpected and unexplainable that no one knew what to do. People in the city stopped talking and stared towards the palace when they heard the news. Elephants gathered together in small groups and looked at each other's feet in silence. A dozen or so mahouts of the royal elephant stables limped into the sunshine and sat on the grass, tending their cuts and bruises. A strange disillusion and sadness floated over the kingdom.

When a messenger was finally sent up to tell the King the sad news, people felt some hope that an answer would soon be found. It was as if the unexplainable could be left alone now. If *anyone* could understand this mystery it would be the King—he loved Scarless Face more than anyone, and had known the elephant since the day he was born.

Yet the King was not completely surprised when he heard the news. A part of him had always feared that something like this might happen, although now that the moment had arrived he couldn't speak, and old fears rushed upon him. He sat down. Through his window he could see the roofs of the royal elephant stables but he couldn't bring himself to look over to where Scarless Face now lay, right below him, exhausted from his anger and pain. He asked himself quietly, *"What could it have been?"*

The King had had a terrible experience once, which he never talked about. It had occurred long ago outside the palace walls. He had never gone into the city or the country since. Some people thought he'd seen too much poverty and suffering and it had frightened him. Some thought the sun had made him go crazy. Others claimed that, as a child, a beggar had grabbed his arm. Either way, he'd never gone in the outside world again. And around the time that he had that experience in the outside world, an elephant was born inside the palace walls. When he visited the royal stables one day, the young King was so moved by the innocence of the baby elephant's face he vowed he'd protect it from all suffering.

"What could have happened?" the King now asked himself. But he was too afraid to face the truth. So he sent for his peace of mind and answer to all difficult situations—a wise old woman who lived very close to God, in a nearby village.

This wise old woman had seen it all, and she had the gift of putting herself into other people's shoes. She was a longtime friend, as close as a mother to the King.

She was a bodhisattva—centuries later she herself would be reborn as the Buddha. But now, having heard the King needed to speak with her, she walked towards the city. She left her village, walking along a path that went through herds of cattle and through fields of sugar cane, and on through large banyan groves. She walked in the shade where beautiful wide sleeves of branches grew down into the ground. One banyan tree was so huge she walked for a hundred yards underneath it, brushing into branches as if she were walking through a herd of still elephants. She smelt all kinds of fruit trees growing just beyond the shade, and went on through thorn-bushes, and out into paddy fields where men and women were working in the sun. At the edge of the city she stopped to talk to people she recognized. Then she entered crowded streets and walked into alleys where many poor people lived. Some were very old, like her, and some just starting out. Some were sick and some were laughing, and children ran among all of them, oblivious. Dogs and chickens stood in ditches, watching her pass. She continued on across a bridge made of boards which crossed a stream and passed a noisy market square. Then she walked up a road that led to the palace gates, which opened up before a marble staircase. She passed guards and walked along a hall until she entered a room with many windows. This was the room where the King did most of his reading, a private space where he allowed himself to think about everything. When the old woman entered the room the King stood up and rushed to her, bending low to touch her feet—and immediately he felt a calmness.

"Something has made Scarless Face go crazy," the King began.

And the old woman, tired from her walk, sat down and listened to the King.

"Don't worry, I'll go see him," she said after hearing his story. She raised her hand in a gesture that had a way of subduing his fears. Though she was sad her old friend was suffering, secretly she was hopeful that this might be the final test that would bring him out of his life of hiding.

The old woman approached the stables and walked directly to the gate of the main stall and looked inside. It was evening now and the stall was so dark that she couldn't see a thing.

She leaned over the gate, straining her eyes to get a good look. She noticed, right in front of her, the motionless body of Scarless Face. The elephant's side abruptly rose up towards her as he breathed. His eyes were half open.

The old woman opened the gate, walked in and sat down beside him. Scarless Face glanced at her, and then stared fearfully back at the ceiling. Slowly, the old woman's presence restored some peace in Scarless Face. He fell into a deep sleep and no one else came near the stables that night as Scarless Face continued to rest.

By sunrise the old woman had left his side.

Before leaving the stables, though, she visited the injured mahouts and asked to hear their stories and if they had noticed anything unusual.

The mahout in charge of watering the elephants spoke first.

"I checked him for bruises and pitchfork cuts, but there wasn't a mark on him . . . "

"True. No one's touched him," said another. "We thought thieves—who were seen one night talking outside his stall—had done something, but no."

The old woman listened and soon was able to make sense of it all. After all, she had lived a long time and she had a way of putting herself into other people's shoes. *Scarless Face is a naive old soul with big ears*, she thought. *His heart is very protected.* She pieced together a story: Scarless Face had heard the rough talk of thieves during the night and had suffered a shock. He was all confused and worried about good and evil. Secretly, the old woman knew this was the best thing that could have happened to the elephant and his King.

So she went to tell the King what she'd discovered.

When the King heard about the thieves he looked out the window pensively.

"What more can I do to keep such characters away from him?" he asked.

The old woman looked at him kindly. "Such characters aren't the problem. Both you and Scarless Face need to go out and see the world. You think you have been protecting Scarless Face and yourself all these years from all that's ugly and evil, but you need to go out of this palace and take Scarless Face with you, and make peace with the world."

The King listened closely. "Is that *really* necessary?" he asked finally.

The old woman nodded and as the King looked deep into her eyes he saw that she was telling him the truth.

He looked out the window. The smell of smoke drifted up to him and he saw small fires in the distance where people were cooking their dinners. He pictured himself walking with the old elephant on an abandoned road near such fires. The two of them going out, lost and hungry, into the night.

"It would only be for a short while . . . and the two of you would keep each other company."

And so, as evening fell, the King went to the royal elephant stables. When he got there Scarless Face was still sound asleep. The King sat down next to this elephant he had raised and protected from birth. Sensing the King's presence Scarless Face moved his face closer to the King's feet and remained resting for a long time.

Finally, before dawn, the King spoke quietly to Scarless Face, and words spiralled into the giant ear and stirred the elephant's mind so that he began to wake. Soon Scarless Face stood up and looked about the stall.

An hour later, with all preparations completed for the journey, the King and Scarless Face, covered in garlands, left the palace at dawn. They walked out into the world and they both lived happily, in suffering and in joy, the remaining years of their lives.

THE CYCLE OF REVENGE

RETOLD BY M.G. VASSANJI

THIS TIME WHEN THE WISE ONE came to their village he was escorted inside with noisy excitement. Unlike his previous visit, which was his first one, news that he was on the road and arriving had reached them several days in advance. Last time he had come as a stranger and taught them hope and forbearance, in the face of drought and despair, and they had accepted him as their teacher. Some even went so far as to call him an avatar of God, but that fact remained to be seen.

The Wise One, in his flowing white robe and white cap, with his long strides, sought the generous shade of the tree under which he had sat before; people came and sat in front of him. He accepted sweet milk in a saucer, and declined to have any more.

"So how goes it," he asked the headman.

"We are in mourning, Lord," the headman said.

Yesterday, even as the excitement was mounting in anticipation of the Wise One's arrival, a man and woman, husband and wife, were discovered dead, having killed each other in the most brutal fashion. They were found with knives, locked together, and gorged on each other's blood and flesh.

Such a deed they had not come upon before, even by armed and ravaging bandits. What beastliness had overcome the couple? How could a man and wife do this to each other?

The people's faces were grave as the event was described and afterwards they looked upon the bright enlightened face before them in expectation.

"Listen, then," said the Wise One after a while. "Hear this story. And ponder."

Many years ago, in a certain village, which could be this one, a boy came of age in a decent hard-working family, and his folks, as is the custom, found him a girl to get married to. The boy had only one other sibling, a sister, older by a few years, and the brother and sister loved each other dearly, having played together ever since the boy was born.

Now, when the new bride was brought home, the sister was delighted at first. But as the husband and wife spent more time together, and exchanged looks and teased each other and went away by themselves, as is the way with young couples, the sister was overcome by jealousy. Because of her age she had become unmarriageable, and consequently miserable and lonely. Where there had been love and devotion there flowed now the bitter poisons of hate and envy and suspicion. In her sister-in-law's every act she saw a scheme to deprive her of her place in the house; in the wife's every act of fondness for her husband she saw an elaborate plan to deprive her of her brother's love. Finally, when her sister-in-law became pregnant with child, her jealousy and bitterness knew no bounds. Now, she imagined, she would be an outcast in her own brother's home, and grow old, scorned and unwanted.

She thought of a scheme of her own.

She feigned affection and solicitude for the expectant mother that was an inspiration to watch. She would press her feet when the pregnant woman was tired, she would fan her when she rested, and she would bring her milk to strengthen her so she could carry the child better. But in the milk she gradually began adding potions to thwart the child's delivery. And in due course the woman miscarried.

When she became pregnant again, the same sequence of events was repeated.

"Foolish woman," the townswomen told the frustrated mother. "How long do you think, while that jealous unwed sister lives in your house, you will carry a child in your womb?"

But the young man, her husband, would not hear ill of his sister. And far be it for him to throw her out into the streets. The woman got pregnant again, but this time she would not accept food from her sister-in-law, who then kept to herself.

One day as the heavily expectant woman lay panting on her mat, her sister-in-law said, "Let me massage you, sister. Why do you think so ill of me? What harm could I do to you, my dear brother's wife, or to his child? As it is, I have nothing else in life but to serve him and his family."

And so as the expectant woman relented, the sister administered a massage using a potent mixture prepared from mustard oil and some roots that can be bought in the area. Under this evil administration, the poor patient writhed in pain and helpless sorrow; as she aborted the child, herself on her deathbed, she breathed out this curse: "Even from death I shall come and haunt you and have my vengeance." And she died.

The poor distraught husband now believed the suspicion his wife had relayed to him and the story the townspeople were frantically whispering. In his rage he killed his sister.

In the course of time this sister was born as a hen, and the man's wife as a cat in the same household. One day as the hen sat over the eggs she had laid, the cat crept up on her and killed her and destroyed her eggs.

In the course of time the cat died and took birth as a sheep; and the hen was reborn as a wolf. And one day the wolf saw the sheep with two lambs suckling from her, and quickly gorged on their flesh.

And so it continued, this cycle of vengeance: one came as a rabbit, the other a hawk; a lizard, a fly; a deer, a leopard.

Now, one day in the grasslands the leopard spotted a herd of deer and gave chase. At the side of one female deer ran its young one and the leopard headed for these two who were among the slowest. And, besides, the meat of a young deer is tastier. But just as the leopard was poised to leap upon his prey, a hunter who was on the scene with many men and powerful guns shot and killed the leopard for trophy and the deer and her young one for meat.

Even so the cycle of vengeance and hatred was not broken; it was merely interrupted by an event of greed and lust.

The leopard took birth as a young woman in a certain village, which is this one; the deer came as a young man in a good home. The boy became a handsome youth. Fate, the deeds of their past, the desire for revenge with which they crossed each of their past lives, brought them together again in a bond of marriage. So long as they prospered they were happy. But came the drought, and the young man's fortunes fell. He had not saved for such an eventuality, and lost much of his land and his standing in the town. The jewels had to be sold, and this earned him the contempt of his wife. He in his turn grew to hate her. Quarrels came like thunder, abuses were thrown like stones and knives. After quarrelling they satiated themselves on each other; and whenever the woman became pregnant she would cause herself to abort only to deny him of a child.

And finally one day, the abuses became real blows and knives. And you know the rest. They consumed each other.

When the Wise One had finished, there was silence. From somewhere came the sound of children; dogs barked; a blacksmith was grinding a tool.

"A rich neighbour has a richer neighbour," said the Wise One. "Misfortunes should not lead to ill-will; envy and revenge are poisons that sink deep into the soul and destroy it. There is no wealth greater than contentment. But contentment is not easy to attain. Every night after the day's ordeals, for a few moments sit down in one place and think about what you have accomplished; where you have come from, where it is you are going, what is the meaning of it all.

"The next time remind me and I shall narrate the story of the lust of the hunter and his gun.

"But I will now rest. After that we shall bury the poor couple."

THE MONKEY AND THE CROCODILE

RETOLD BY RAJ RAMANATHAPILLAI

ONCE UPON A TIME, a monkey and a crocodile lived in a thick jungle. The monkey lived on a huge naval tree, which was situated beside a big river. The crocodile lived in the river. The monkey was a happy one because the naval tree gave more than enough fruits. The naval fruit is a tiny purple fruit. It is very sweet with a delicious taste and a wonderful smell. The monkey had the whole huge tree to himself. However, he loved to share the fruits with the crocodile who lived in the river. So they became great friends. Almost every day the monkey climbed to the top branch of the tree, picked the biggest naval fruits and threw them into the river so the crocodile could eat them. The crocodile was always pleased with his monkey friend's generosity. In the evenings they spent a good deal of time talking to each other. The friendship of the monkey and the crocodile grew day by day.

The crocodile always took a share of naval fruit to his beloved wife. She too enjoyed the delicious fruit—to the point where she became addicted. One day she thought, "If the monkey eats this fruit every day, would not its flesh be tastier—especially his liver?" Now she really wanted to eat the monkey's tasty liver and her mouth always watered whenever she thought about the monkey. One day she expressed her wish to her husband and asked him to bring the monkey to their home so she could eat the liver. The husband was so upset and worried. He explained to his wife how much he loved his monkey friend and how important it was for him to maintain his friendship with the monkey. He argued that it was impossible for him to kill his dear friend who was generous enough to share his fruit with them.

The lady crocodile was not convinced and she became very angry with her husband. She demanded that her husband bring the monkey to her so she could eat his delicious liver. If he did not, she threatened, she would leave him. The husband was torn apart inside. He did not want to lose either his wife or his friend. However, he did not have much of a choice but to lose one of them. With great difficulty and pain he decided to lose his monkey friend. So he swam back to the river shore and rested sadly under the tree.

Seeing his sad crocodile friend from the top branch of the naval tree the monkey immediately came down to a lower branch and asked, "My dear friend, why do you look so sad?"

The crocodile said, "Oh, it's nothing. I am just a bit tired. By the way, I wonder whether you would be interested in going for a ride on my back? I could show you the beauty of the river."

"No way!" said the monkey. "First off, I could never go for a ride on the back of a crocodile, and what's more, I am afraid of the water."

"Well," the crocodile said, "haven't we been friends for a long time? It would be a shame if you didn't trust me by now. Furthermore, you don't need to be afraid of the water when you are on my back since I am, after all, King of the River. So trust me. There can be no life without trust."

The monkey thought for a minute.

"Okay, I trust you," he said, and he leapt joyfully down from the tree and onto the back of the crocodile.

They went on a long ride. The monkey was enjoying the ride and was terribly excited. But the crocodile was quiet and deep in thought. After observing the crocodile for a while, the monkey said, "What's the matter?"

The crocodile almost burst into tears. "I am very sorry, my monkey friend. The main reason I am taking you for a ride is not just to entertain you, but to take you to my wife."

"Is that true? I am so delighted to finally meet your wife. Why didn't you tell me this at the beginning?"

The crocodile felt more pained. "My friend, it is not going to be a social visit. To tell you the truth, she wants your liver."

The monkey was confused. "Why would she need my liver?" he asked innocently.

The crocodile replied, "Well, since you eat the delicious naval fruit, she believes that your liver must be very tasty . . . therefore she wants to eat your liver."

The monkey saw his life was in danger. Within seconds he thought of an escape.

"Oh my poor friend, is that all that you were worried about? I have no problem giving my liver to your wife. I would be honoured, in fact. But you should have told me about this matter before we left the tree."

"Why?" asked the crocodile.

"Well, usually I clean my liver with water and then put it on a branch of the tree."

"So what should we do now?"

"It's not too late, my friend. If you take me back to the tree, I'll give you and your wife my tasty liver."

The crocodile was happy and swam quickly to the naval tree, with the monkey holding onto his back. When they reached the shore the monkey jumped onto the tree with relief and immediately shouted back at the crocodile:

"Hah! Crocodile!—Don't you know I can't take my liver out? This is a good lesson for me about whom one should trust."

GARUDA AND THE SNAKE

RETOLD BY GRIFFIN ONDAATJE

IT WAS AN INCREDIBLY HOT day. A festival had attracted thousands of people to the river. By early morning many of them had arrived at the edge of the water, their shadows arriving behind them, their colourful reflections floating ahead of them like birds near shore. Most of them walked into the river and then turned and walked along the shore and moved on towards the temple.

Gods were there too, among the cows, dogs, humans, elephants, goats, snakes and birds. They would nod to other gods and then find a place to sit or stand. For the most part, though, their presence, standing in the shade of an elephant or sitting on stone steps that led down into the water went unnoticed. Occasionally they'd cup a handful of water and cool their skin.

On this crowded shore it was still possible for people to stand in the quiet of a daydream. Someone would look up at the horizon, or look down at a step in front of them, and then images, invisible to anyone else, would begin to flow into their head and be recalled like a part of life they had forgotten. Then their shoulder would be bumped by someone, or a toe would rub their ankle and they'd wake and see the river flowing in front of them.

By chance a snake and a giant bird were standing close to one another, observing the events of the day from the same spot along the river. In the bustling crowd it wasn't easy to see who was standing beside whom and, because he was tired from his day's journey, and because he didn't think it would be a big deal, the snake decided to lean over and rest his neck on the person in front of him.

This person happened to be a garuda bird.

The garuda is ancient and powerful, and just as eagles and hawks are true enemies of snakes, he is even more so. He hunts all snakes, poisonous and non-poisonous alike. He also eats them, even at social gatherings, and keeps his eyes roaming for them.

Garuda turned to see who had placed a hand on his shoulder and was surprised to see a snake there, staring dreamily into the crowd.

The snake, at the same moment, turned his head in a casual way to see who he was leaning against. To his shock he saw that the shoulder belonged to Garuda. Frightened to death, he fell, his body dropped to the ground like water poured from a bucket. He hit the ground and slid quickly down the hill into the river.

Just as quickly, Garuda's wings popped up above the crowd like dark umbrellas, and he hopped and flew, aiming to catch hold of the snake as they went down the hill and out across the water.

Now, about a mile downriver, in a leaf hut, lived a hermit. He was at this moment standing in the water, up to his stomach, trying to keep cool while soaking his old shirt in the water. He planned to put a robe of bark on top of this shirt later on. He was a kind hermit who had eyes like a daydreaming child and he talked to himself as he swept his arms in wide circles about him, trailing the shirt in the water. When he looked up he was startled to see a commotion of two figures in the distance, splashing towards him.

The first thing his eyes made out was a snake's head zig-zagging down the river. It swam frantically, like a dog with its head straining above the surface. When this snake saw the little hermit standing by the shore it turned in his direction, twitching its tail to escape Garuda's claws.

Garuda, meanwhile, bobbed up and down angrily, just behind the snake. His huge wings touched the water, his long claws scratched the surface, as if trying to run on the river.

For the little hermit who stood watching, waist-deep in water, the snake and the garuda appeared like a terrible vision from one of his dreams. And even though they looked strange, and very frightening, the need of the snake was not lost on the hermit. So the hermit remained as fearless as possible in front of the bird and the snake— who now headed directly for him. Each time the big wings lowered, the snake would speed forward on the surface, and in this way the two resembled a strange row-boat, with dark oars and a serpent's head jutting forward at the prow.

Just as it entered the shallows where the hermit stood, the snake magically transformed itself into a green gem, and bounced over the water. It bounced up on shore and struck against the hermit's bark robe—sticking there like a clump of mud.

So as not to collide with the hermit, Garuda spread his wings to rise above the shoreline of the river. He flew in a wide circle and then slowly glided down to the shore near where the holy-looking man stood in the water. Garuda had seen where the snake hid itself and he stared hungrily at the green stone stuck in the robe, but, out of reverence for the hermit, he wouldn't move towards it.

Garuda pulled in his wings and addressed the hermit:

"Sir . . . please excuse me distracting you like this . . . but I am very hungry. And I must tell you that in your robe there is a gemstone that is not a gemstone. I'm here to inform you that this gem is actually a dangerous snake who has disguised himself very cleverly in order to escape me. I tell you this because I saw the transformation with my own eyes, and, after chasing him for miles down this river, I would like to eat him. In respect for your way of life, however . . . I could wait until nightfall, when he sneaks from his hiding place and tries to flee across the ground."

The hermit smiled and lifted his hands out of the water. He let his shirt float on the surface as he put his hands together and greeted the giant bird. Then he spoke clearly:

"You've decided to spare this life for my sake, even at a time when you find yourself very hungry. Although you chased this serpent and meant to kill it, you should feel blessed for your decision to resist harming him. I am honoured to witness this moment. I hope this is the beginning of a time when you will never again need to feel hungry in this way."

Garuda was confused. He didn't know what these words meant. He wasn't sure what to say now, and didn't want to show disrespect by repeating himself. He glanced quickly at the gem in the robe. Perhaps the hermit hadn't understood and yet, when Garuda hurriedly reviewed his own words, it seemed that there was nothing missing.

A minute passed.

Neither of them spoke.

Garuda stood on the shore, blinking and staring at the hermit, who stared back at him. His heartbeat began to slow down and the day also seemed to become strangely still. He felt the damp sand of the shore sink underneath his tensed claws, and the tips of his wings were dripping with water—he hadn't noticed this before. He looked down into the current of the river, which was as clear as wind. There were some minnows pointing upstream, small blades of grass were slowly wheeling past them in the current, bending like palm fronds in a storm. In the air he breathed he suddenly felt glad for the way sun and wind mixed together and the way they cooled and warmed his neck feathers. He was intrigued by the river. When his eyes focused on the surface he saw his own reflection there. He thought of standing in the cool water, like the hermit.

When he looked up the hermit was smiling at him.

A little unsure of himself, Garuda stepped quietly into the river. His two skinny legs looked like old arrows that had fallen out of the sky and stuck in shallow water.

The hermit kept smiling. He drew his shirt off the water and waded to shore, touching Garuda's wing as he passed.

The hermit walked over and stood next to the bark robe that was lying on the ground. He leaned down and spoke quietly for several minutes to the snake. Finally he coaxed it out of its hiding place.

The snake's eyes were dark and unaccustomed to the light, but when they saw Garuda so close by, their dark pupils shrank and the eyes changed into a bright green, the colour of grass. The snake stilled his heartbeat as he looked over at Garuda's feet and the terrible sharp claws. He looked at the enormous beak on Garuda's face, and then at the black wings which almost touched the ground. The snake was ready to flee again—but the hermit spoke:

"Such a beautiful day it is today. The sun's so bright. You both could join me at my home further down the river. We could all sit . . . ."

Neither Garuda nor the snake said anything. So the hermit kept himself busy, moving back and forth along the sand, gathering sticks and cleaning his shirt and his robe. Occasionally he stopped working, stood quietly and exchanged smiles with his new guests.

Several hours went by.

The snake lay close to the water and Garuda leaned his weight on one foot, staring at a patch of weeds.

Eventually the sun began to set. The snake realized he had been dozing off and he woke up suddenly. Garuda had been sleeping too and he raised one eyelid slowly and turned sideways so that he could observe the sun. When the sun went down behind some trees the two creatures looked at the hermit to see what he was doing. They could see he was still smiling away and they realized the invitation was still in the air.

The hermit yawned, picked up his personal belongings, and started to walk home. He called out to them but neither knew how to reply. The hermit was leaving without them.

Without a word the snake and Garuda decided to follow the hermit. Soon all three of them were moving along the shoreline—Garuda stepping in slow, exaggerated steps over grass, and the snake, with his bad eyesight, following slowly at first and then moving quickly enough to bump upon the heels of Garuda.

When they all arrived at the leaf-hut, the hermit sat them down and told them about the blessings of love and kindness. He talked and talked. The snake and the bird listened, and then the two of them exchanged a few words about the weather and the fine tea they were drinking. They listened closely to each other's comments and nodded slowly, staring at one another across the campfire. The hermit resumed talking again as the cooking fire burned its kindling down to the ground. Then they all became quiet and gazed at the glowing wood until their eyelids felt heavy.

After a few minutes the hermit lay back on the ground and fell asleep.

The snake moved closer to the warm ashes of the fire. Encircling himself, he gently rested his head in the soft dust. He looked over at Garuda on the other side of the campfire. Beyond the bird's silhouette the snake could see tiny, out-of-focus stars. Garuda's two eyes suddenly opened and floated there among the stars. He stared back down at the snake.

For just a few moments, while the hermit slept, the two of them looked deep into each other's eyes, until they seemed to be watching their own reflections. Then they looked away and glanced into the dark.

They heard the hermit snoring quietly. The snake looked over at him and made a little hissing laugh, and Garuda bobbed his head, smirking.

They listened and heard the sound of the river going past them in the dark. Then they looked back at one another, mumbled goodnight and went to sleep.

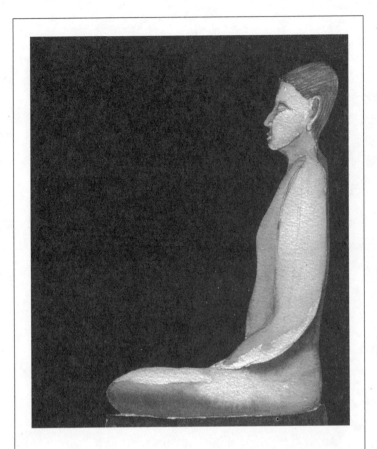

JUST LIKE THE REST

RETOLD BY GRAEME MACQUEEN

Who art thou, whose outward appearance is that of an animal,
while thou willingly perform deeds of mercy?

Hans Christian Andersen,
The Marsh King's Daughter

ONCE UPON A TIME a king ruled in Benares. In itself this was not unusual. Kings of Benares have been many. In fact, since time has neither beginning nor end both the kings who have ruled in Benares in the past and those who will rule there in the future are beyond counting. Kings of Benares have sometimes found this fact depressing. A king, after all, may not wish to be just another king of Benares: he may want to be special, to be noticed, to be remembered. He may want stories to be told about him. Perhaps it is this yearning to be special that leads to the development of unbalanced behaviour in kings of Benares, or even in kings in general? In any case, we may suspect that the king in our story owed his immoderate behaviour to such a yearning, for his parents made the problem worse by naming him Prince Just Like the Rest.

When he became king, Just Like the Rest concentrated all his energy on one thing: hunting. He was an exceptionally big man, and likewise strong and fleet of foot, and hunting gave him the opportunity to show off these qualities. He was intent on making it clear to everyone that he was a great hero, the model of masculinity. Other men, he intended to prove, were not men at all. So it was a case of hunting in the morning, hunting in the afternoon and hunting at night. It was hunting here and hunting there, while law and statecraft could go to the devil, and did.

One morning King Just Like the Rest thought of a way to make the day's hunting even more pleasurable than usual. He assembled his courtiers and said:

"Today, a miss is a crime. Anyone who has a chance at a deer and lets the deer escape will be regarded as having broken the most weighty law in the kingdom and will be punished accordingly."

Since the King's wish was law his courtiers had no choice but to go along with the plan, but they were not happy. Perhaps their station as mere courtiers led them to have lower expectations than the King and hence more balanced behaviour? Anyway, there is no evidence that they wanted stories told about them. They gathered secretly and said to one another:

"This king will be the death of us. Why, even the finest hunter may have a bad day. There are days when a man may spit in the sink and miss! Let us agree that if a deer comes our way today we shall do our best to make it run in the direction of the King. In this way he will be the one forced to try the shot and we can keep ourselves out of danger."

While it was still early morning the King ordered the hunt to begin. Deep into the forest went his men, and they formed a large circle around an area where deer were known to take refuge. Heavily wooded was this spot, difficult to penetrate, favoured with streams and thickets. Taking out their swords, the men beat the flats of the blades against tree trunks. They thrashed the bushes with their staves, drummed on the ground with their feet and, raising their voices in hair-raising cries, made a perfect racket. Hardly had they begun their noise-making when an enormous stag rose up from a thicket and tried for his freedom. His body was great and dark like the shadow of a cloud and his antlers were like the branches of an oak. The men trembled to see him. But, fearing the King's wrath and the day's proclamation, they held their positions.

As the stag made for the circle he saw how things stood. Shoulder pressed shoulder, bow rubbed against bow, sword rattled against sword. It was a circle of death. So back towards the thicket he leapt, and he raced three times around that thicket, the wind in his antlers like the moaning of a storm through tall trees. The first time around the thicket he was afraid, for it is the nature of deer to fear those who pursue them. The second time around he was confused, for it seemed to him that he was destined for something higher than to be hunted. The third time around he remembered who he was. He was the Great Being, the one headed for Freedom, the one who would become the Teacher, the one who would help the world to lay down its burden, the one who would dry the world's tears. And with memory came courage, for he thought, "This is not the way I shall die."

When the men saw the stag head resolutely for the circle a second time they knew that he would not turn back. Those on either side of the King turned quietly aside and left the King exposed, aiming to cause a break in the circle so that the stag would take this as his route of escape. Indeed, the stag sized up the situation at once, and, perceiving a heroic figure in gorgeous clothing standing by himself, thought, "This must be the King." He made straight for him. The King fitted an arrow to his bow and took aim, although the stag's gaze felt like hot sand in his eyes. He let loose the arrow.

Now, I must tell you that the deer of these forests are far from helpless in the face of bowmen. The parents of these deer teach them all about arrows, which they refer to as Birds with Four Wings. They teach their young numerous strategies for avoiding arrows, such as swerving, bouncing, flinching, flouncing, soaring in the air and rolling on the ground as if hit. The Great Being had in his present lifetime fully incorporated this teaching and, considering carefully his options, decided on the roll. Down he went as if struck a death blow, down with a clatter of hooves and antlers, down like a stack of kindling collapsing. The King, seeing the white belly twitching in the grass, threw back his head and cried: "A hit! A hit!" And all the men in the circle, neglecting their formation, rushed to the deer echoing, "A hit! A hit!" No sooner had the hunters lost their concentration than the stag was on his feet and running like the wind. He passed so close to the King that the King could have put out his hand and touched him if he had had the presence of mind.

Except for the sound of the stag crashing through the forest, there was silence. No one dared to speak. Then someone was heard to mutter, "What poor fellow has let the deer past him? I would hate to be in his boots."

And another said, "For a moment it looked as if the deer was headed towards His Majesty."

"If it were not impossible," added a third, "one would conclude that His Majesty had missed."

"But," said a fourth, "not only is it impossible that His Majesty should miss, but we must bear in mind that His Majesty distinctly said, 'A hit! A hit!' And His Majesty is incapable of deception."

"Fair enough," put in one of the King's courtiers, "but His Majesty did not specify the object of his hit. Possibly he had in mind a sapling, a clump of grass or even the air?"

"That is it," they all began to cry in unison. "The air! The air! The King has struck the air a good one, he has taken it in hand, made sure of it, fixed its wagon! Warriors! Men at arms! The air is dead, long live Just Like the Rest!"

Now, the King was neither simpleton, fool nor idiot. Perceiving that he was the object of a display of wit he grew angry and, standing in the centre of the multitude and raising his arms, said in a loud voice:

"Today we shall see who should be numbered among fools. This stag will be dead before the sun reaches its highest point, and I shall kill it without the help of any of you!"

So saying, he turned on his heel, drew his crystal dagger with his right hand, and plunged into the forest on foot after the stag.

No man could run like this king. To run deer to the ground was a pastime for him. For four hours he sped through the woods in close pursuit, leaping fallen trees and brushing aside dense growth that would have brought another man to a standstill. Yet the stag he chased was no ordinary stag. It was the Great Being, whose strength, speed and determination came from countless lifetimes of self-sacrifice. It was not easy to catch the Great Being intent on his freedom! And so it was that after every heroic leap or sudden burst of speed the King succeeded only in catching sight of the stag as it disappeared behind the next hillock.

"Soon," thought the King, "the sun will reach its zenith. I must make a great effort to take this deer." Just then the stag was approaching a flat, circular place in the woods, empty of trees but green with weeds and vines. Avoiding it, the stag ran around its rim. The King saw his opportunity. He cut directly across the green, intending to intercept the deer on the other side. If you had been at the scene you would have seen the King flying over the weeds one moment and in the next moment you would have seen no king at all! Great would have been your astonishment!

Now, this is what happened. A giant tree, the uncle of all banyans, had once stood on the spot that was now choked with vines. Struck by lightning, it fell over on its side, its great roots torn from the earth. Over time both tree and roots had rotted away, leaving a pit that was half filled with rainwater and hidden from view by the tangle of growth. Twenty yards deep was this hole, and it was filled with water to a depth of ten yards. In this water the King now fought for his life. Sheer were the walls of the pit, and slippery with mud. Not the tiniest root or stem grew within the King's grasp.

The King was in trouble. His size could not save him, his strength could not save him, his speed could not save him. His boots, inlaid with silver, cat's-eyes and lapis lazuli, were of no use to him, and with much effort he got them off and let them sink to the bottom. His elaborate royal headgear, flashing with jewels, went the same route. Then down went his sword, famed among kings and reputed to have been forged by Vissakamma, and his crystal dagger, gleaming like the morning star. Finally, he struggled out of his heavy leather clothing, worked with gold and set with the clearest gems of Kasi. This king was as naked as at the moment of his birth.

Weariness crept over him. Alone and failing, unable to recall from his past a single pure deed to buoy him up, he prepared for his end, uttering this verse:

> The sun is high.
> The King goes down
> to join his useless
> sword and crown.

At that very moment a shadow closed over the King, and looking up he saw, framed by a tangle of vines, the stag, standing over the pit and blotting out the sun. "He has come to taste his victory," thought the King. But it was not so. After he had gazed silently at the King, the stag went down on his knees. (The tree spirits were stunned, the serpents of the forest watched.) Down on his knees went the Great Being and bent his head into the pit. As he knelt the woods went quiet. There was calm throughout all the planes of existence. Even the beings in the hells felt a relief from their agonies. There had never been a silence like this in the history of the present aeon.

Down stretched the spreading antlers of the stag, and the King closed his tired hands around the tines and felt himself drawn up to the light.

The King retained only a dim awareness of what followed—of being hefted onto the broad back, of being carried to the edge of the forest, of being found by soldiers of his army. But that evening, when the King was clothed again and dining in the splendour of his palace, the chief priest noticed a change in him and saw that there were tears in his eyes.

Next morning, the priest, being concerned about his king, went to the royal bedchamber at dawn, and he saw the King awake and sitting at the head of his bed, his legs drawn up as if he were meditating. And he heard the King speak these words:

> An illusion of living,
> a pit, a drowning.
> A sense of silence,
> someone kneeling.

"Surely," thought the priest, "His Majesty has been transformed." And it was true, for there was no hunting that day or the next. Instead, the King took an interest in the righteous administration of his realm. He encouraged people in acts of integrity and mercy. Astonished, his people responded like parched plants to rain.

Years went by, the King's beneficent rule growing in depth and extent, till one day, Indra, king of the gods, noticed a change in the universe. It came to him first as an intuition of fullness, a sense of an increase in the ranks of the gods. A sort of divine population explosion.

"Amazing!" he thought. "Positively out-of-the-way! The number of gods increases daily. What can be the cause of this?" So he investigated, and he discovered that the new gods had been men and women in their previous lives, and that they came from a region of the world dense with goodness. The centre of this region was Benares.

Now, Indra is well meaning but something of a busybody, and in cases like this he enjoys nothing more than to throw on a disguise and put somebody to the test. So, descending to Benares, he took on the form of the chief priest and accompanied the King while he took his daily exercise in the forest. The King, you see, had never given up his love for the forest, or for the bow. He enjoyed setting up targets and shooting at them. So Indra created a magical illusion of the great stag and had it stand directly between the King and the target.

"There he is," whispered Indra in the excited voice of the priest, "the stag who humiliated you long ago. Here is your chance to even the score! Shoot, Your Majesty!"

"Impossible," said the King, lowering his bow.

"But you are a man, and hunting is a man's work."

"Not possible," said the King.

"You are a king, and venison is the food of kings."

"I will not," said the King.

"Your Majesty, I am the chief priest of the realm, skilled in the reading of signs and portents. I assure you this is no ordinary deer. It is the deer that brings good fortune. Kill him and you will win mastery over the people of the world, mastery over even the gods. Let him go and you will experience rebirth in the hells, and your friends and family with you."

"Then let hell welcome me," said the King. "And let my friends and family—and you too, priest—accompany me. For I shall not kill the one who saved me."

At this, the stag vanished and Indra threw off the priestly disguise and appeared in the air in his own form, shouting in a charming voice, "Well done! Well done, king who has passed the test!" People for miles around heard the sound and saw Indra in the sky. He was so shining and beautiful that those who looked directly at him fainted or fell in love. Some did both simultaneously. Others, who had been taught about such things by their parents, wisely looked at him through smoked glass, or regarded his reflection in a small drop of water held in the palm.

Indra said many praiseworthy and pious things that day about the stag and the King, but no one remembers any of them because he was too beautiful to be taken seriously.

On the other hand, people have remembered that king, as is clear since you are reading this story. Perhaps, after all, there is something to be said for unbalanced behaviour. And the people of the realm changed the King's name to More Just Than the Rest.

THE RUPEE

RETOLD BY S.M. LENA

LONG LONG AGO, there lived a young fool in a village in India. He was a carefree young man, healthy and strong.

The headman of the village was very rich. However, he was a typical miser. One day he had to go to another village carrying with him a large sum of money and much gold and jewellery. The gold was part of the dowry he had to pay to a family in another village in order to finalize the marriage of his daughter.

Between the headman's village and theirs, however, there was no road—only a narrow jungle track winding through the trees. The headman realized he would have to hire someone to accompany him on this dangerous journey. So he thought about it, and decided it would be wise (and economical) to hire the services of the young fool.

The young fool readily agreed to go with him for a very small fee. He tied the one rupee coin he received as an advance to the front of his sarong.

On the way, as night approached, they found themselves still in the middle of the forest. They decided to sleep for a while and continue the journey in the morning. The headman walked away from the footpath and lay down and went to sleep behind a thick bush. The fool looked about himself lazily, then stretched himself across the path and fell asleep too.

A short time later, a gang of robbers happened to come that way. The leader of the gang tripped over the fool. Mistaking him for a log of wood, he called back to his men to be careful of the log lying across the track.

The young fool, suddenly wakened, took great offence at being called a log of wood. He got up and shouted, "How dare you call me that! Have you ever heard of a log of wood that sleeps happily with a brand-new rupee coin in its lap?"

The robbers were taken aback at the appearance of this man. They looked at one another. Then one of them stepped forward and asked if he could see the coin. A dispute followed over the genuineness of the rupee.

The young fool was even more insulted by the insinuation that this rupee was not a real one.

"I'm an honest man! And this coin is genuine," cried the fool. "If you doubt my word, ask the headman of my village. He's sleeping over there, behind that bush."

Needless to say, the headman was woken up and quickly relieved of all the gold and jewellery he possessed.

IS THE RIVER ASLEEP?

RETOLD BY SARAH SHEARD

THERE WAS ONCE A TEACHER who travelled everywhere with four of his best students and because they were never apart they eventually began to attract some notice in the land. Whether the teacher was unbelievably stupid or actually a genius of some perverse kind became a matter of vigorous debate amongst people who encountered him. Wisdom sometimes disguises itself heavily and no one likes to make mistakes in these matters. Of his students, however, there was no doubt, and so the group came to be called the Completely Stupid Teacher and his Four Foolish Disciples.

One day this teacher was invited to travel on an assignment to a faraway town. He told his students to pack food and clothes and get ready to accompany him, which they immediately began to do. "Oh, another trip, a trip!" they said, bumping into one another in their haste and excitement until they were grouchy and bruised, surrounded by chaos, and Teacher had to go to his room and rest.

After some delay they began their journey, travelling without incident until they came to a river bank. The river wasn't too wide but it had to be crossed if they were going to get to their destination on time. Disciples looked at Teacher; Teacher looked at disciples. No one wanted to be the first to speak and possibly say the wrong thing, although with this group there was little chance of avoiding that. Finally, Teacher spoke. "My learned pupils," he began. (Like all great teachers, he knew the value of encouragement.) "I ask you, is it safe to cross this river?"

Everyone stared hard at the river as though hoping it might answer for them, and, in fact, just then a little ripple, raised by a passing breeze, broke across its glassy surface. The eldest student, convinced this was another of Teacher's trick questions, knew how to answer. Looking into the distance, he cocked an eyebrow and said, "I'd be cautious here. Calm rivers can often be the most treacherous."

"Yes, absolutely," chorused the others, all eyes on their teacher.

"Yet we must get across," continued the first student. "So tell us how, Great Teacher."

Annoyed that the question had bounced back to him so soon, Great

Teacher picked up a twig he'd found at his feet and began to scratch his head. His greatest insights often came while scratching, under pressure. "Obviously, this river can only be crossed when it doesn't know we are doing so."

His students nodded sagely, utterly mystified.

"Otherwise," he continued, "we will be drowned, carried downriver and our bloated bodies torn apart by village dogs some days hence."

The foolish pupils wished he hadn't added that.

"But how will we know when it's the best time to cross?" asked the persistent eldest pupil, not to be put off by such imagery. His teacher shot him a stern glance as though the answer were too obvious for words. "Aha! We'll have to cross the river when it is asleep!" the student replied, terribly anxious to be recognized as Teacher's brightest student.

"Yes, but how do we know if the river is sleeping or not?" another pupil spoke up. An idiot can always be found in the crowd to make things uncomfortable for leaders. The ambitious pupil glared at the one who'd spoken but he was forced to admit it was a valid question. Teacher scratched some more and then flung his twig into the river and they all watched it drift slowly downstream. "It's obvious," he said, "this river is not some little guy we can pinch to see if he jumps. We'll have to use the burning log test." He smiled in exultation, pleased to have hit on something practical.

His pupils immediately set about producing a burning log for him, hoping not to be asked what came next. Three of them gathered firewood while the fourth pulled together some rocks and in a little while they had a tremendous bonfire. The senior pupil handed the biggest log over to their teacher and watched while he crept down to the river bank and plunged it into the water. There was a great hiss and a puff of smoke that made them jump out of their sandals. "Shhh," said their teacher. "Let's try again at midnight."

The five of them tiptoed around making camp, humming all the lullabies they knew, sitting on the river bank, swaying, shoulder to shoulder, to help put the river to sleep. Eventually they too lost consciousness, snoring in one another's ears until the stars came out and Teacher woke them with a shake. Creeping on his elbows and knees down to the shore, he picked up the log and dipped it in the water once more.

Silence.

Tucking their clothes up above their knees and piling their possessions on their heads, they crossed the river to the other side.

They were wringing out their shirt-tails, intensely relieved to have survived without mishap, when a peculiar thought struck the youngest pupil. "Have we truly all arrived?" he mused, half to himself. The seriousness of this question slowly dawned on them all, for it was a known fact that people could lose themselves crossing devious rivers in just this fashion. The youngest pupil began to count but could only come up with four people. Knowing his weakness at numbers, he asked the eldest pupil to count again, and again it came out to only four! In a frenzy they all began furiously recounting, including Teacher who, at hearing a chorus of "fours" but no "fives," shook his fist at the river and began to howl. The others, seeing that, joined in and their tears formed damp spots on the fronts of their freshly dried shirts.

A passerby, drawn to the wailing, came up and inquired what the matter was. Through his tears and gestures, Teacher conveyed the reason for their distress and the passerby smiled, for he had heard of this famous troupe of idiots. He raised his hand. "Stop. Do you want to get your fifth man back?" The weepers lifted their heads as one and choked in mid sob. At last, an easy question.

"We would do anything," their Teacher said, "to have our number restored to us."

The passerby smiled a curious little smile. "You must be prepared to suffer, but if so, I guarantee your friend will be found."

At this, he broke off a willow branch as thick as two fingers, stripped the leaves from it and bent the first pupil over. "As each of you feels the blow, shout out a number," and he gave the first pupil a great whack with his stick.

"One!"

The passerby bent the next pupil over and gave him a blow and continued down the line until he came to their teacher. He was given the biggest whack of all. "Five!" shouted Teacher with a roar, and tears both of happiness and pain coursed down his ancient cheeks. The pupils hugged one another with inexpressible joy at having recovered their lost party. They thanked the passerby with all their hearts, thumbed their noses at the river and continued on their way.

HANUMAN AND SITA

RETOLD BY RAJIVA WIJESINHA

THE MONKEY HANUMAN was the son of Vayu, the god of the winds. He could change himself, too, into whatever shape or size he wanted. It was these factors that helped him to find Sita, when she had been stolen away to Lanka, by Ravana the Demon King.

Sita's husband, Rama, the exiled prince of Ayodhya, had no idea where she was. He and his brother Lakshman searched for days before they found Hanuman and his friend the monkey prince, Sugriva, who were able to show them a scarf that belonged to Sita, wrapped around her earrings. She had dropped it to them as she passed across the skies above them, borne in Ravana's arms.

But where she was to be found, and how she was to be recovered, no one knew. First Rama had to help Sugriva conquer Vali, his half-brother, and take over the monkey kingdom. Then Sugriva sent armies to north and east and west to search. And to the south he sent the largest army of all, bears as well as monkeys, commanded by his son, with Hanuman to guide them.

After many days they came to the southern tip of India, where the three seas wash across each other endlessly. There the army stopped, bewildered. The distance to Lanka was over a hundred leagues—more than any ordinary bear or monkey could leap.

"Unless," said the old bear Jambavan, "the son of the wind tries—with the help of his father."

"I'll do it," said Hanuman.

He went backward till he came to the first of the Malayalam hills, so he would have firm ground under his feet. Then he grew larger, and the muscles in his legs began to swell—and suddenly he had jumped, and covered half the distance across the sea, and then he was gliding, gliding gently down the wind, and getting smaller, as he floated smoothly down into the foothills outside Ravana's grand capital, the great city Maha Nuwara.

He was in a valley, where spices grew in profusion and fruit trees flourished and the air was full of wonderfully mingled fragrances. He plucked some mangoes and ate them and began to understand why, wherever Ravana went, whatever he conquered, he always came back to Lanka.

"But I am not here to stay," he sighed, "I have to find Sita. But still—I will have to wait till nightfall."

So he stretched himself out where a stream fell gently through pools of rock, and he slept. It was night when he awoke, and he changed himself into a cat, with gleaming eyes, and began loping his way steadily up through the hills, through the northern gates of the capital, and into the citadel itself. As he walked through the night the noise in the streets faded. The bazaars closed down and the lights went out one by one as the people retired into their houses. By the time he came to the palace doors, only the sentries were still awake, standing two by two at all the doors.

Hanuman crept between their legs, scampering away if they saw him and tried to chase him away or to pet him. At last, having wandered through long, brilliantly lit corridors, he came to a heavy door outside which four sentries stood. This, he thought, must be the king's bedroom.

He made himself smaller still and fluttered through the keyhole in the form of a mosquito. What he saw overwhelmed him. The countless wives of the Demon king were asleep in disarray, bright and beautiful in the moonlight that streamed in through the open windows. Hanuman flew above them looking to see if Sita was amongst them, hoping that she was not.

Finally, at the end of the room, he came to a crystal bed on a dais. There lay Ravana fast asleep, his ten heads arranged elegantly on the raised pillows. His twenty arms stretched in all directions, but in the two strongest he held the most beautiful woman Hanuman had ever seen.

Could it be Sita? Hanuman had never seen Sita before, and he was frightened. He fluttered closer to look, and the woman stirred, and lifted up her hand to slap at him, and he realized that this could not be Sita. She would have understood that no creation of nature would seek to harm her. It must, he realized, be Mandodari, the daughter of illusion, Ravana's queen. Sita must be safe.

Hanuman flew over to the window sill and then, once more a cat, slithered down into the courtyard below, through the feet of the sentry who was gently nodding in the fragrant air. The courtyard was bare, paved with squares alternately black and white, and Hanuman knew this must be where Ravana played chess with men and women as pieces.

But where did the scent of spices and fruit come from? Hanuman looked all around him, and at the end of the courtyard he saw a gate leading into a dark grove. He padded in that direction and went through the gate, and then he heard a noise, soft and suppressed, that he knew was that of a woman crying. It must be Sita.

And so it was. She was sitting under a peepul tree, thin, worn, not half as beautiful as the daughter of illusion had been. Around her, at some distance, twelve old women sat, horrid, with matted hair, some of them asleep, some watching her, some looking up at the moon above them.

Hanuman changed himself into a little lizard, and scuttled along the ground and up Sita's arm. Her tears stopped for a moment, and she held out her arm and studied the lizard sitting there, its head perked up, its eyes bright.

Hanuman wondered what to say, so that she would not be frightened and so that she would trust him. Suddenly it struck him that he had known all along.

"Rama, Rama," he said, and he saw Sita's eye light up and she smiled. "I am Hanuman, the son of the wind. Rama sent me to find you."

Sita held out her fingers and he crawled into her hand, and she turned to the tree and placed him on it. Her back was now to the aged demons.

"I knew you would come," she said.

"I can take you back," he said. "Climb on my back, and I will get you away at once."

"I know you could," she said, "when you have changed your shape again. But I must wait till Rama comes and rescues me himself, openly. He has to overcome Ravana first—not for my sake, or for his own, but for all the worlds."

They talked through the night, of Rama, and of the kingdom of Ayodhya, and the other kingdoms of this world, and of other worlds, and of Rama again, until the stars faded and the first light began to appear in the East. And then—

"You must go now," said Sita. "And tell Rama where I am, so he can come for me. But first, make your presence known, so that Ravana will realize the time is coming soon."

"But what should I do?" thought Hanuman, as he slipped away.

When he reached the courtyard, he had decided. Nothing should happen near Sita, to disturb her peace. Instead he sped away to the gardens at the back of the palace, where benches were set under shady trees, where fountains played and vines crept up trellises. There he resumed his normal form, and grew larger, so that he could uproot benches and trees, fountains and trellises, and fling them one after another onto the roof of the palace and through the windows.

Ravana heard the noise in his bedroom; but before he could give any order, the sentries had responded, and they rushed from all corners into the garden. Hanuman uprooted the biggest tree of all, and swung it at the first and the second and the third pair who approached, and smashed them into the ground. The rest stopped.

Ravana realized that something more was needed. He sent a message to Jambumali, the son of Prahastha, his chief general. Jambumali had been trained in the magic arts, and he had a special arrow that he shot right up into the air as he came to the edge of the garden. Then he waited.

Hanuman saw him, and felt sorry for him, for it was his first battle. But it could not be helped. He uttered his own magic manthrum, and the arrow, twisting at the top of its trajectory, turned back as it came down, faster and faster, pushed by the wind, as well as by its own speed. Almost before Jambumali knew what was happening, it had cleft him in two.

Ravana, meanwhile, had gone to his son Indrajith who was meditating. Magic, he knew, was useless. It was the power of the spirit that was needed. Indrajith sighed when he was told, but he agreed, and from where he sat he sent out an arrow with the noose of Shiva flying behind it. As the arrow touched Hanuman, the noose wrapped itself tight around him. He would never have been able to free himself.

The bodyguards rushed at him too, when they saw him fallen, and tied their own bonds around him; and when other bonds are attached to Shiva's noose, it loses its power. Indrajith, coming out, saw what had happened and sighed again and went back to his meditation.

Hanuman knew that he was free to go if he wanted, but he wanted to see Ravana too. He let himself be carried into the throne room, where Ravana sat, trying to decide what he should do.

"Who are you?" he asked. "Why are you dressed as a monkey?"

"I am a monkey," Hanuman replied, laughing. "I am the son of the wind, and the messenger of Rama. I have come to ask you to give Sita back."

"How did you get here?"

"I jumped."

Ravana grew angry. "If you don't tell the truth, I will have you killed."

"It is the truth. And you cannot kill a messenger."

"I can do anything I like."

"But you mustn't." It was Ravana's brother Vibhishana who spoke. "There are some rules even you cannot break."

"I've broken them before."

"That's when I wasn't here. Now I tell you that you mustn't."

"Let him go," said Prahastha. "Let Rama come with an army. Then we can show them what we're made of."

Ravana frowned. "All right. But punish him, set his tail on fire, carry him around the city so that everyone can see him, and then throw him out. Let him jump into the water to put out the fire."

Hanuman smiled to himself, and waited until the bodyguards had slung him on two poles and carried him outside. He waited till they had wrapped his tail in oily rags and set it on fire. And then, as they tried to lift him up again, he leapt away and careered through the city, setting fire to all the buildings he passed. The wind fanned around his tail, keeping it cool and helping the flames to spread.

When he felt he had done enough he leapt back into the palace compound, bounded through the garden so that he could quench the flames in a fountain, and went back into the grove so he could say farewell to Sita.

"Give this to Rama," she said, dropping a pearl into his hand. "It is one of the pearls my father tied into my hair on our wedding day. I will give him the other when I am rescued."

Hanuman bowed and sped away. He leapt over the walls of the city, into the foothills, and again onto the dry plain to the north. And there he grew even bigger and the muscles in his legs swelled again, and once more he jumped over the sea, and was gliding down the wind, until he was at the cape of the maiden where the three seas wash across one another endlessly.

"I have found her," he said.

"Go and tell Rama at once," said Jambavan.

"No," said Hanuman. "We will go back as we came. Extra powers should be used only when they are necessary. There is a time and a place for everything."

So they went back as quickly as they could. Rama was sick with anxiety by the time they reached him, for all the other armies had returned with no news. But he revived when he heard from Hanuman about Sita and the messages she had sent him.

But how he readied an army, and how they built a bridge across the ocean, and went to Lanka, and fought until the demons were vanquished and Sita was won back—that is another story.

ANGULIMALA

RETOLD BY MICHAEL ONDAATJE

The fletcher trims the arrow shaft.
Water carriers guide a river through gardens
and through places of drought.
The carpenter shapes wood.
The wise one tames the self.

I WAS TOLD THIS.

The Buddha was teaching in Savatthi—that great grey city with a hundred gates and a hundred guards. In the region at that time there were known to be two rulers: there was the King, and there was the thief—Angulimala—a vicious robber, a murderer without mercy, who made villages into non-villages, families into non-families, slaughtering them and cutting off and wearing their fingers in wreaths round his neck. (Angulimala means "a garland of fingers.")

Each day the Buddha taught in the town and slept on the outskirts overlooking the plain. One day he decided to travel through the country that he saw every morning when he wakened. As he was leaving, people kept stopping him—cowherders, cigarette makers, local publishers, municipal guards, goatherders, bandicoot trappers, some loose women, some loose men.

"No. No no. No no, sir, not this way, dear Holy One, down the road is the bloody-handed thief, the murderer. He has made villages into non-villages, turned towns into non-towns, and families into non-families. He murders them all and wears their fingers around his neck. If people travel they travel in large groups. And sometimes even these ones fall into his hands."

But the Holy One ignored them.

Later stilt-walkers, potters, lime-burners, out-of-work politicians, other goatherders warned him.

"He has made villages into non-villages, he has—"

"Yes, yes," the Holy One said and went on.

He carried his bowl. He was wearing just his robe. And no one went with him. When he left the edge of the plain and stepped into the forest he was approached by ancient hermits as he passed their caves. Some recluses who disliked sunlight and stepping on roads came towards him with difficulty.

"He has turned families into non-families . . . ," they moaned, vaguely remembering their families with sentiment. "He even wears their fingers . . . has sewn them into a coat! A coat of fingers! Excuse me, Your Holiness. But Angulimala means 'a garland of fingers!'"

"Ah yes," the Holy One said and persuaded them away and went on.

As the Buddha crested the hill above the Plain of Kosala, Angulimala saw him. He stood in the shadow of his trees.

He thought to himself, "Usually I am approached by armed groups who think they can protect each other. Twenty, even forty, travel together, and even then I overpower them and murder them one by one. (Just last week I murdered the Completely Stupid Teacher and his Four Foolish Disciples.) But this foolish monk ambles alone, bravely, as if he were a conqueror in disguise, a king, a planetary stranger. I think I'll kill him."

He took a sword, a bow and arrow, and began to follow him.

But the monk seemed to always stay ahead, magically. He could not be overtaken, no matter how fast the murderer walked or even ran. He seemed to be just ambling along, carrying his bowl, holding the hem of his robe to avoid the dust.

"Remarkable!" said Angulimala to himself, feeling suddenly very alone. "I have caught elephants, deer, horses, even that group of acrobats from the circus, but I cannot overtake this damn monk!"

So he gave up. He stood there and yelled. "STAND STILL WILL YOU! STAND STILL. I WANT TO TALK TO YOU!"

The monk turned.

"I am standing still, Angulimala, so why don't you stand still."

"But that monk is walking," Angulimala thought to himself. "He's walking and he says he's standing still. What the hell is he up to? These monks are supposed to be truth tellers."

He yelled back, "*What the hell do you mean?*"

"I am standing still, Angulimala. I've abandoned the use of force against living things. You act against the living without any restraint, racing after this, racing after that. You are always trying to catch up and turn living things into ghosts. You never stop. I am standing still and you are not. You chase and kill even in your dreams while the world around you moves at a quarter of the speed you do, and so you will die far sooner than the world around you."

The words pierced Angulimala and he was still. At last a speaker of truth had entered his forest. This was a great and sudden journey, surrounded by silence, like a stone falling and falling into a well.

"I will bury my evil," he said quietly to himself.

He dug a pit and covered his sword and all the other weapons. Then he approached the Holy One and he bowed low to him and touched his feet.

He asked how he could serve him and how he could some day become a disciple. And Buddha, the Compassionate One, the teacher of the visible and the invisible worlds, said, "Come then . . . monk."

2

And so the slayer of villagers and pilgrims and families became a monk. The two of them travelled on together, Angulimala accompanying the Master. When they returned to the outskirts of the town of Savatthi, Angulimala said farewell.

He returned to the forest and lived there alone. He had an old robe and a bowl and sometimes he would enter the city to beg for alms. He became aware for the first time of the suffering around him. He witnessed the poor and those without homes, those in pain, the fear in young children. He saw the victims of political wars and brutality. He was discovering how tormented we are.

The next time he entered the town for alms he was recognized. A thrown rock hit him in the chest. Someone else flung a piece of metal at him. Then others were throwing sharp flakes of pottery towards him so his face and feet were badly cut. They rushed at him and beat him and tore the robe he wore into pieces. They smashed his bowl and then they began to break his fingers until he fainted there on the street. They threw dead animals over him and tried to bury him in the corpses of dogs and birds. They spat at him and pissed on him and left him there like that.

He woke up in the darkness with a crow's beak jammed against his mouth. It was hours later. There was no one in sight, no light. He could sense the still pulses of the animals that covered him. He pulled himself out of the mire of bodies, unburied himself, and he walked out of the city.

As he entered the forest he saw the Holy One and he half crept towards him in pain and humiliation. He was embarrassed to approach him like this. He sat some yards away from him, bleeding, his robes in rags, facing his Master. His Master smiled at him. And then even chuckled with him. And finally spoke.

"Endure it, Noble One. Your past evils which would have driven you towards hundreds of years in dark and airless hells have been briefly experienced by you, here and now."

Then the Holy One lifted the man who had been a murderer to his feet and walked with him till they found a river and he bathed him. He gave the murderer his own robe and his begging bowl and he left him there. Angulimala came in this way to understand the joy of freedom. And, in the stillness that surrounded him, these verses came to him. And he began to sing.

> The fletcher trims the arrow shaft.
> Water carriers guide a river through gardens
> and through places of drought.
> The carpenter shapes wood.
> The wise one tames the self.
> Some control with sticks,
> some with money and guile,
> but with none of these

was I tamed by Him.
I was a thief,
I was the Violent One,
notorious as "Garland of Fingers."
I was the Great Flood.
I had a future of a thousand evil rebirths
when I came to the Buddha for refuge.
I had performed acts of such terror.
But now I move in the freedom
of spiritual carefulness.
So we complete
the Buddha's teaching.

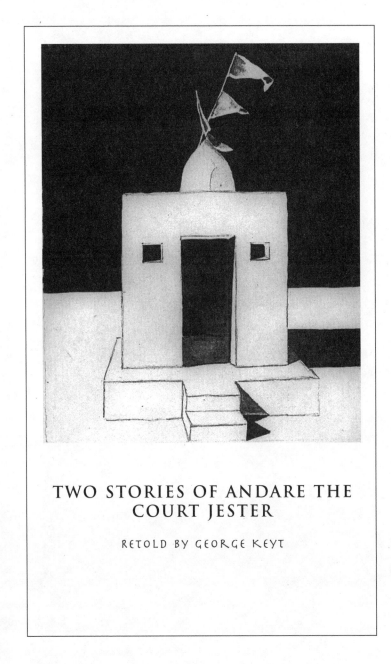

TWO STORIES OF ANDARE THE COURT JESTER

RETOLD BY GEORGE KEYT

THERE WAS A COURT JESTER called Andare whom the King and Queen liked very much. He could always go and see the King in the palace even when he was not called to make him laugh, as was the way with court jesters.

One day while Andare was walking about in the palace grounds he saw people putting out great heaps of white sugar on mats to dry. He looked at the sugar and felt like eating a lot of it. So he stood thinking for a little while and then went to the palace. He knew where the King would be and went there and saw the King and made obeisance to him.

The King smiled and asked, "What is it, Andare?"

Andare said, "Your Majesty, while I was walking in the palace grounds I saw people spreading out great heaps of some white stuff like flour on mats, but it was not flour, it looks more like sand. What is it, Your Majesty, and what is it for?"

The King sensed Andare knew it was sugar that was being dried, but thought a while and said, "I suppose, Andare, it must be white sand for scattering on the garden paths." Then Andare took his leave and went away, saying that his wife was sick.

He went home and told his son that he must come to the palace grounds where white sugar was being spread out in the sun and shout and say, "Father, Mother has died!" When Andare had gone back to the barns of the palace where the sugar had been put out on mats, his son came running and called out, "Father, Mother has died!"

Andare inquired, "What, my wife has died?" and the son said, "Yes, Father, she has died."

Then Andare loosened his hair knot and let his hair stream down. He pulled off his shawl and threw it away and wept loudly and called out and cried, "Then it is better that you and I eat sand. My poor wife! Then it is better that both of us eat sand," and he caught his son and they both fell down and rolled about. They went rolling onto the mats with the sugar crying, "It is better that we eat sand," and Andare began to push handfuls of sugar into his mouth and that of his son.

When this was told to the King he laughed and said, "It is one of his tricks. His wife is very much alive. He wanted to eat the sugar and that is why he came to ask me what the sugar was."

***

A little way from Andare's house a landlord of the village had a kitul palm tree in his garden. When the kitul tree was in flower, he tapped it and hung a pot there to catch toddy. He went every evening and took the toddy. Andare came to know of this and he climbed the tree in the morning before the landlord and drank the toddy. But he climbed with a bag slung over his shoulder and a sickle stuck in his belt.

When the landlord went afterwards to get his toddy he saw that there was very little left in the pot, and thought, "There is some thief who comes here and drinks my toddy. I must catch him."

So he went very early the next morning and hid near the tree and kept watch. Andare came with his bag slung over his shoulder and his sickle tucked in his belt and climbed the tree and drank the toddy.

He had almost climbed down when the landlord came out suddenly and shouted at Andare, "What is this you are doing, climbing up and down my kitul tree?" Andare replied, "I have not done anything. I only went up the kitul tree to cut grass." The landlord got very angry and shouted, "Are you trying to play the fool with me? How can there be grass on a kitul tree?" and Andare replied, "That is why I came down from the tree. I saw that there was no grass there." And he walked quietly away.

THE ROAD TO BUTTERFLY
MOUNTAIN

RETOLD BY MANEL RATNATUNGA

Long long ago, it is said, there lived two brothers. The elder brother was a pious man spending his time in religious pursuits. The younger brother was married to a girl with unscrupulous morals.

This girl tried her utmost to seduce the elder brother. Failing in her attempts she scratched herself violently one day and reported to her husband that the elder brother attacked her.

The husband, believing her, ran in search of his elder brother. He found him reading his *Sathipattana*, the text of mindfulness, in the forest near by.

The younger brother ran up to him, abused him in rage and hacked off his brother's hands and feet.

The elder brother fell onto the forest floor.

"I'm not angry with you," said the pious brother through his excruciating pain, "only please lay my book on my chest."

"Lay it yourself," responded the younger brother and returned to his wife.

An aged woman who had come to collect firewood in the forest discovered the bleeding elder brother and took him to her home. She tended him with great compassion and healed his wounds.

One morning the King's royal tom-tom beaters were heard making an announcement.

"King Bhatiya's flowers are being stolen nightly by thieves. Anyone who can catch the thieves will be handsomely rewarded."

The tom-tom beaters added:

"The King's gardeners, his infantry, his cavalry, have all endeavoured to catch the robbers and failed. The King is sad. He is a lover of flowers. Someone is so daring as to rob him of his finest flowers every night."

The elder brother, listening from the old grandmother's hut, said to the tom-tom beaters:

"Take me to your king."

Everyone laughed. But the drummers led the cripple to the King.

"Your Majesty, if you build me a hut near your most fragrant flower beds, I will try to catch the thief," said the cripple.

King Bhatiya commanded his prime minister to supply the cripple's needs. They erected a hut near the white jasmine bush reeking of perfume.

The cripple spent the night reading his *Sathipattana* in a melodious voice. He read on and on deep into the night. In the wee hours before dawn the cripple heard the peal of silvery laughter.

The cripple went on with his recitation.

"Tell it louder for us to hear too," voices said outside his closed door. "Open the door so we can come in."

"I can't," said the cripple. "I have no hands or feet."

"Here," said a sweet, tinkling voice, "here's the edge of my sari. Let it touch your body."

The cripple saw a beautiful gossamer cloth slip in through the door. He reached for it.

He had a strange sense of shock. He found himself with hands and feet again.

He opened the door but did not release the gossamer sari edge in his hands. A flutter of gorgeous goddesses came floating into his hut. They were carrying golden baskets loaded with white jasmine from the King's garden. But the goddess whose sari he held could not move.

"Please release my sari," she said sweetly.

"Not until you tell me why you steal the King's flowers," said the elder brother, now no longer a cripple.

"Our flowers fade when we bring them to earth to worship the Buddha's footprint on Samanala Kanda," said the trapped goddess.

"The Buddha's footprint on Samanala Kanda? Where is such a mountain?"

"It is where the butterflies go to die. I will show you if you let me go."

"Show me first; then I will release you," insisted the elder brother.

The other goddesses laughed their silvery laughter and floated out of the hut and away. The trapped goddess pleaded, "There is no time now. I must go before dawn breaks through. See, my friends have already gone. My friends and I will make a flower road for your king to find. Tell him to walk along it. It will take him to the footprint of the Buddha."

The elder brother released her sari and the little goddess flew to join her friends.

Next morning, at the elder brother's request, the King with his mother, his ministers and his people went in search of the flower road.

It was easy to find. The King's fragrant white jasmines were strewn across the city, along the rice fields, and through forests up a steep mountain seven thousand feet high.

Up and up they followed the strewn flowers, through a dense tangle of tropical foliage infested with snakes and leopards and the black bear. No one had dared invade this mountain forest before.

Higher and higher the King and his following went, panting as they climbed. As night fell, the people lit the way for the King and his mother with giant firebrands.

At daybreak they crested the mountain peak. There, as told by the goddess, was the footprint of the Buddha. It was true.

The footprint was covered with a large crystal to protect it from the harsh monsoon rains.

King Bhatiya, his mother, his people, the elder brother, fell on their knees and touched the footprint with their foreheads.

The King, as promised, gave the elder brother much treasure.

Climbing this mountain rising sheer from the centre of the island has become a romantic pilgrimage undertaken by the citizens at least once a lifetime. Trekking is done by night to reach the peak at dawn.

Buddhists call the peak Sri Pada. Christians and Muslims call it Adam's Peak. The Hindus believe the footprint belongs to Shiva.

So all religions converge on Samanala Kanda, the butterfly mountain.

A CHANGED SNAKE

RETOLD BY DAVID BOLDUC

IT HAD BEEN A HOT DAY. The sky, which had been a blazing yellow glare for most of the afternoon, was now blue and in a few moments when the sun touched the horizon it would change again to a cool watery pink. People were beginning to move about, the green, rose and orange saris of the women at the village well glowed like neon in the fading light and children played noisily among the huts as the blue smoke from many cooking fires twirled slowly into the still air. In the distance a holy man with matted hair and beard, dressed in a simple saffron-coloured robe and carrying an iron trident, picked his way slowly among the many paths that wound through the fields. Now and then he would make his iron staff ring against a rock, enjoying the clear bell-like sound it made in the still evening air.

At the same time, underground in the cooling earth a snake, roused by the ringing sound, woke abruptly from his dream and moved towards the fading light. He was big—about six feet long. He had a vicious reputation and he was not terribly bright. His habit of terrorizing the villagers, killing their children and decimating their flocks had not left him a lot of time for meditation, and outside of his usual routine of attacking and biting he tended to have a hard time getting things straight. At the moment he was hungry and that awful ringing in his ears had given him a headache. His mood was sour.

Clang, ring! Clang, ring! Along came the holy man lost in the sound of iron against stone. *Clang, ring!* Out came the snake, a pain in his head and murder in his heart. And they met.

The snake reared up angrily, hissing his fury at having been disturbed. He swayed back and forth in front of the holy man like a knife fighter looking for an opening. Time seemed to stop.

The sun moved a little lower. The holy man, on seeing the snake, leaned casually on his trident and focused his watery eyes on this angry creature who was obviously suffering the effects of a deprived childhood or two. By this time the snake was hissing and ducking and weaving. The holy man didn't seem to understand—in fact, from the snake's point of view, it appeared as if the holy man was hardly paying attention at all—but, just as the snake began to move in for the kill, the holy man leaned down and held out his hand, saying:

"If you'd like to take a bite out of me, please go ahead."

Now nobody, not *anybody*—animal, vegetable or mineral—had ever offered the snake anything, ever. Nobody had ever cared enough about him to show him the slightest consideration or offer the least comfort (there were good reasons for this, of course, but these were lost on the snake). He was overwhelmed. He was still moving in on the holy man, hissing dangerously with lips curled back to reveal long, sharp fangs—when the holy man's generous offer touched him and the world began to spin before the snake's eyes. As his teeth were about to sink into the monk's hand—he recovered, swayed back and with a voice he hardly recognized as his own replied, "No thank you." Then he fell back as if struck to swish and swirl out of control in the dust at the holy man's feet.

The snake had responded to kindness. He was impressed by the monk's gesture. He was also impressed by his own out-of-character response. He had responded to kindness—now he wished to be kind. His well-placed, or ill-timed, response (he still wasn't sure which it was) to the holy man's largesse showed him that at least once, in a past life, he had been a little further up the social scale. He was impressed, and in that moment the holy man had placed the seed of ambition within him. It was up to the snake to work it out.

After a bit, when the snake was able to pull himself together and some of the dust had settled, the holy man gave his iron trident a ringing clang against a rock and the snake got up, coiling as he rose, until he supported himself gracefully before the monk. He waited.

The holy man, turning from his trident, crouched down so as to be able to look right into the snake's eyes. The snake became lost in the holy man's gaze and, for him, time stopped. The sun touched the horizon and it seemed as if he were in a dream, hearing the holy man say, "Don't bite and you'll be all right."

Standing up and stretching the kinks out of his back, the holy man gave the snake a smile and then left.

The snake was already strengthening his resolve for the task ahead, but he felt that he could use a bit more information—not to mention some encouragement.

"Hey!" he shouted after the holy man, but the holy man was gone.

The snake was eager to enter into his new life and like many new converts he was eager to share his good fortune with his friends. Yet this was not to be, for his friends were just like him, the old him, and unfortunately for our hero they felt that you were either a real snake or a real victim—and furthermore they believed that anyone talking the kind of stuff the snake was talking just had to be a real victim. When they were through with the non-violent snake they were certain that they were right. The snake made no converts: he barely escaped with his life.

Once he had recovered from his friends' attentions the snake was off down the path to the village. After all, he thought, the villagers aren't snakes. He had reformed; surely they could respect that. We will all be friends, he thought.

As for the villagers, they had suffered for years because of the snake. They didn't like him and they didn't want to be friends with him. But they did welcome the opportunity to get even—and get even they did. The poor snake paid dearly for keeping his mouth shut, though to be fair it wasn't as if those villagers didn't have their reasons. And so it went; every time the snake would venture out into the world, with sealed lips, the world would beat him like a gong. Where once people had gone out of their way to avoid him they now went out of their way to beat him.

A month passed. It was a long month for the snake, who now lay curled up numb and dumb in his lair trying to figure out if the monk's words had some hidden meaning. The words had seemed plain enough before and he couldn't, for the life of him, see any riddle now. But he was certain that the true meaning of the holy man's words still eluded him. The meaning had to be eluding him, otherwise he wouldn't be black and blue all the time. Anyhow, apart from a headache, he wasn't gaining anything from thinking about it. And then the ground shook in a familiar way—*Clang ring! Clang ring!* And he knew that up there, close by, was a holy man, maybe *his* holy man. So he dragged his cracked and bruised body up out of his hole and onto the path.

The holy man, the same one, was startled by the condition of the poor snake.

"Have you had an accident?" the holy man asked.

The poor snake was so happy to see the monk that he kept nothing back, and the more he told of what had happened to him since giving up biting, the more upset he became. He was about to tell it all a second time when the holy man reached over and patted him gently on the head.

"And when you hissed, didn't it scare your attackers?" asked the holy man.

"*Hiss?*" said the puzzled snake. "I didn't hiss."

"But my dear fellow, I said *not to bite*, I didn't say not to hiss."

The poor snake. Earlier he had felt hurt and now he felt stupid, but before he could say anything the holy man was once more on his way.

The sun was close to the horizon and the smoke from a dozen or so fires was twirling into the cool blue air. The snake, hissing, returned to his burrow, feeling that at least life had not passed him by.

AKBAR AND BIRBAL

RETOLD BY GRAEME MACQUEEN

AKBAR THE GREAT was the Emperor of India. He was large and strong and had a fine beard. He loved life, he loved laughing and he loved manly pursuits. Pursuing deer, for instance, and elephants, and tigers. Tigers! Now, they were worthy opponents. Akbar had once wrestled a tiger for twenty-three minutes, and although the match ended in a draw he had won great renown. He wore the claw marks from that fight with pride, and people bowed when they saw them. The deepest scar began at his hairline and ran right down the middle of his face and throat, disappearing under his tunic. It made him look as if some jinn had tried to divide him in two and failed. Or perhaps the jinn had succeeded and Akbar had put himself back together! Akbar called this line The Divide, and he liked to say that it helped him distinguish his left side from his right.

Akbar had a counsellor named Birbal. He trusted Birbal completely, even though Birbal did not go in for manly pursuits. Birbal liked to say that he already knew his left from his right and needed no reminder.

One day Akbar thought up a plan for manly entertainment. He smiled and showed many teeth when he thought of his plan. Heroes from all over India would come to his capital, and there would be pleasure, renown and a good time for everyone.

Now, the Yamuna is a famous river flowing down from the snowy Himalayas. It passed right by the Emperor's palace in Agra and it was cold enough to chill your bones. So this was the plan that Akbar devised: all the heroes who accepted his challenge would wade into the Yamuna up to their chests clad only in loincloths, and the one who stayed in longest would win a hundred gold pieces. It was clear and straightforward. And when one of Akbar's counsellors remarked that it sounded easier than wrestling a tiger, Akbar smiled and said, "You will see the Yamuna's claws soon enough."

The contest was announced throughout the Mughal Empire, and long streams of men flowed towards the palace from all directions, their armour and weapons glittering in the sun. They were of noble birth and they sought fame and the Emperor's favour.

When the day of the ordeal approached, the men began preparing themselves, each according to the latest theory. Some had their servants rub ladle after ladle of sesame oil into them, convinced this would shield them from the cold. Some ate pints of almonds, following the teaching that almonds warmed the blood. Others swallowed quantities of gold leaf, adhering to the theory that the gold would accumulate in the stomach and radiate heat like a furnace. And some relied on years of idleness and rich living, thinking that their plumpness could now be turned to good account.

On the fateful day the contestants lined the shore for four miles, each with a crowd of family members, followers and lackeys. Oil was poured, almonds were swallowed, gold leaf was placed on outstretched tongues. There was music, flattery, prayers and epic verses. It was all very inspiring.

Unnoticed in the crowd walked a thin, serious man. He was alone and his clothing was simple and well worn. He was a stonemason, and he had a very sick daughter. The gold pieces could spell the difference between her life and her death. His family did not know of his plan and he spoke to no one. He had no oil, no almonds, no gold, no fat. He stood for a long time looking at the Yamuna.

At noon Akbar arrived in high spirits and gave the signal to begin. His eyes shone. Such wonderful, oily heroes! He shook his head and laughed out loud. The Yamuna would find them tasty.

The warriors waded up to their waists, cheered on by their supporters. Some went laughing, some put on fearsome frowns. Many struck heroic poses in the water, standing with feet wide apart and arms folded over their broad chests or thrusting their fists into the water and shouting as if fighting demons.

The stonemason walked in to the required depth and stood there. He looked at the palace.

Akbar seated himself on a magnificent seat under an umbrella, shielded from the sun. The first hour was exciting, the second hour was long in passing, the third hour was dismal. He yawned and returned to the palace for a nap. "When the sun goes down," he said, "the Yamuna will make its move."

Sure enough, when he came back after sundown he saw families all along the shore wrapping their heroes in long blankets. There was much sighing, much comforting, some crying. Hot drinks were prepared over fires. Only a hundred men were left in the Yamuna and no one was shouting or punching the water. Some stood still and some flapped their arms slowly up and down like large sad birds who knew they were not going anywhere.

Not far off, the palace loomed in the darkness, its windows lit by torches. The stonemason kept his eyes on the torches.

Akbar smiled and went home for a game of chess. He returned to the river with his counsellors just before dawn. The Yamuna rolled on in the grey light. It had lapped up almost every hero in India. One man stood in the water, two others were struggling to reach the shore. The two were rescued by their supporters, who splashed in and lifted them out of the river. All along the shore there was weeping and groaning and crying aloud. It sounded like a battlefield after a night of warfare.

As the sun rose, everyone watched the lonely figure in the Yamuna. Who was he? Was he alive or dead? Slowly, the man took his gaze from the palace and turned his face to the shore. It was the stonemason. Step by painful step he approached the shore, and when he reached it he fell down like a stone.

"Who are you?" people asked, but there was no answer. Akbar looked at the thin, dark figure on the beach and felt suddenly tired and old. One of his counsellors stepped up to the stonemason, looked down at him, and said, "One must admire his pluck. But perhaps his aspirations ran too high?" And he turned away, thinking that he was dead.

But Birbal took off his cloak and put it over the stonemason. Then he rubbed the man's arms and chest until he opened his eyes.

"Was I the last to leave the Yamuna?" whispered the mason.

"You were," said Birbal.

Soon Akbar was back in his palace, staring into a large fire. His counsellors came into his presence.

"The contest is over," said Akbar, with his eyes still on the fire. "We must award the prize."

One of his counsellors stepped forward. "Begging your indulgence, Majesty. Surely the prize is not to be presented to the stonemason?"

Akbar's eyes came into focus. "Why not? He won."

"Majesty, I beg you to consider. These people are not like us. Cold, hunger—these things mean nothing to them. They live with them all the time. They do not feel them the way we do. Majesty, the fellow cuts stone. He hacks away at it, it is the only opponent he has ever known. It is said that one is only as good as one's opponent, and he is therefore no better than a stone. Majesty, a stone is no hero. It will bring great shame to the throne if a prize is given to such a one."

A second counsellor spoke from where he stood:

"One may go further, Your Majesty. One may tell a second truth about the man's ability to withstand cold. One may tell whence he drew his heat."

Everyone turned to look at the speaker, who paused for a moment and then addressed everyone in the room.

"Did you not see this fellow standing like a pillar, with his gaze fastened on the radiance of the royal residence? Was he not absorbing its splendour? Did he not draw on the royal heat, the royal glory, the warmth of the Imperial Majesty? Was not his humble being brought to a white-hot heat by His Highness?"

The counsellor paused again, and then went on:

"To whom belongs the prize? Do we thank a stone for its warmth when it is heated by the sun? To His Majesty belongs the prize, not to this borrower!"

There was a hush, and then everyone began to nod. How could one disagree with such reasoning?

Akbar was uncomfortable. The man's words did not sound right to him. On the other hand, the sight of the stonemason lying like a dead perch on the beach had not seemed right either. Where was the heroism? It had been a disappointing end to the contest. He felt cheated. He stroked The Divide on his face and looked around for Birbal. Birbal was nowhere to be seen. Curse the man, how could he disappear just when he was needed? Just when the Emperor was having trouble telling his left side from his right!

"Go away, all of you! I need to consider these things," shouted Akbar.

Akbar was tempted to go and find a tiger to wrestle. Wrestling tigers was such a simple thing. It had a yes-or-no quality to it. You lived or you didn't. It did not give you a tense feeling in your stomach.

"Go and get Birbal," he said to his attendant. Birbal lived next to the palace, so it was only a few minutes before the attendant returned with his message:

"Birbal regrets that he must first eat his supper of beans."

"Curse the man a second time," said Akbar, but he respected Birbal so he put in a good stretch of time pacing the floor before sending the attendant again.

"Birbal asks your indulgence, Your Majesty," said the attendant, "but he must first eat his beans."

Akbar stared at the attendant, fingered The Divide and said nothing. But when a third summons met with the same reply, Akbar exploded:

"Not acceptable! Not appropriate! Is the Emperor of India worth less than a plate of beans?"

And he strode to Birbal's house, pulling at his beard, his guards doing their best to keep up.

"Birbal! Come out at once! How dare you shame me?"

Birbal came to his door and took Akbar by the hand. "Your Majesty, insult is not my intention. It is just these beans. I have been waiting for them to cook. Does not even an unworthy man like myself have a right to feed his body?"

"Birbal," said Akbar, trying to keep calm, "there is not a bean in God's world that needs this much time to cook. What are you trying to do to me?"

"Come, Your Majesty," said Birbal, and he drew Akbar to his verandah where a pot of beans was sitting in the open, next to the palace.

"Behold my beans!"

"Birbal," pleaded Akbar, "have you, God forbid, been drinking spirits? Or have you overworked in my service and lost your mind altogether? THERE IS NO FIRE UNDER YOUR BEANS!"

"Fire, Majesty? These humble beans have been placed by me right beneath the palace walls! They are drawing on the royal heat, the royal glory, the warmth of the Imperial Majesty! These humble beans are being brought to a white-hot heat by Your Highness! I expect them to come to a boil at any moment."

Akbar looked at Birbal for a long moment. Then he threw back his head and laughed. He laughed and laughed. Drawing the bag of gold pieces from his pocket and wiping away his tears, he said:

"Give this, my friend, to the stonemason. He has faced stone and he has faced water, and they are worthy opponents. May the Most Merciful bless him. And may He bless you too, for to you He has revealed the difference between the left side and the right."

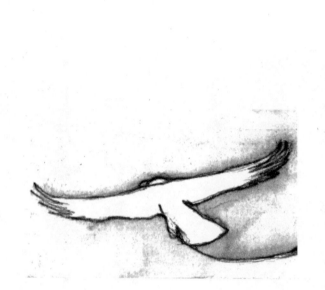

MOUTHFUL OF PEARLS

RETOLD BY JUDITH THOMPSON

A YOUNG WOMAN NAMED SONJA was walking alone at night in one of Toronto's ravines, when a man emerged from the bushes. Sonja glanced at him and, not wanting to show him fear, continued walking at the same pace. He followed, and soon caught up with her, walking alongside her. He then moved in front of her and blocked her way.

Sonja: Excuse me.

Man: Yes?

Sonja: Would you let me pass?

Man: Sure, sure, no problem. I . . . just I saw you and I was just wanting to know if you knew about that . . . part.

Sonja: Part?

Man: Down in the ravine. The more secret part, right? You know that part? It's very nice. I think you'd like it.

Sonja: Please, don't touch me.

Man: I just thought I could take you there.

Sonja: No, thank you, I'm enjoying my walk.

Man: It's not too far out of your way. Come on.

Sonja: Please don't touch me.

Man: I'm not gonna eat you. What's the matter?

Sonja: I would just like to continue my walk, if you don't mind.

Man: Well, why not walk with me? I'm the best walker around. I could show ya parts of the ravine I bet you never seen. Marsh grasses growin' twenty foot high, and wildflowers with colours you don't see anywheres else, magenta, burnt yellows and oranges splittin' and splittin' their gooey white juice.

Sonja: Thank you, but I would like to walk alone. Take your hand off me, please.

Man: Alone? What are ya, nuts? There's real bad guys out there, you know, just waitin' for a loveliesque woman like you. So softy-nice.

Sonja: I don't feel I need protection, and I like my own company. Please let me pass.

Man: Wait a minute, just wait a minute. You don't like me
'cause you think I'm down and out, but you got it all
wrong. Oh yeah. Listen. I could give you more than you
ever dreamed of. I gotta deal I'm workin' on, a big big
deal, I been workin' on it for two years now, it's a muffin
business, ya see muffins are the thing, all the businesses,
the hospitals, the cafeterias all around the city they're
after the big muffin, the perfect light, tasty, the healthy,
the low fat the oatmeal and apricot and the money is
going to rain on me, babe, just rain on down. So stick
with me, babe, you'll have a mouthful of pearls.

Sonja: Let go of me, and listen, listen to me. I'm not interested.
I'm not interested in any of that. I had it. I was vice-pres-
ident at the TD Bank, pulling in 500,000 a year; I had a
house in Forest Hill, a farm in Caledon with a guest
house, an ex-husband, a summer house in Chester, Nova
Scotia, two children, a nanny, a full-time housekeeper, I
read the R.O.B. and nothing else, everything, everything
was acquisition. One day, about five years ago, it was
around seven thirty, I got home from work, I was in the
kitchen, chatting with the nanny, playing with my kids,
and my four-year-old, Julia, she'd been balancing on the
kitchen chair, and it fell backwards. She hit her head on
the dog's food bowl and she was screaming and crying and
I ran to her and she pushed me away. She cried, "I want
Felice," that's her nanny, and she wouldn't let me touch
her. And then, that night, my son Michael was having a
bad dream, about draculas and he cried for Felice. I went
in and sat on his bed and he slapped my face and he cried
inconsolably. The next day I quit my job. I had to sell the
house and now we live all together in one large room.
The kids love it. They say it's cozy, like living in a nice
hotel room. We all watch TV in bed together and read
stories and snuggle and have a great time. My sister's with

	them now. She comes so I can walk and think and know who I am. Do you know who you are?
Man:	You have kids?
Sonja:	DO YOU KNOW WHO YOU ARE?
Man:	I'm a lover.
Sonja:	Where is your soul? When do you feel it?
Man:	When I seen you. Your beauty made it rise up.
Sonja:	That is not about your soul.
Man:	Come here.
Sonja:	No, I will not come there. I'm going to continue my walk. Good night.
Man:	I said come here.

He grabs her.

Sonja:	What is it you want from me, exactly?
Man:	You know what I want.
Sonja:	No. I don't.
Man:	I will toll upon your belly.
Sonja:	What?
Man:	I will toll, like a bell, upon your silver white belly.
Sonja:	Let go of me.
Man:	Will you marry me?
Sonja:	Let go of me now.
Man:	I want to dress you in lace and bone china and kiss your pretty green eyes over and over.
Sonja:	My eyes aren't green.
Man:	Crazy eyes.
Sonja:	You want my eyes.
Man:	Lookin' at me. Lookin' at my body. I been workin' out, you know. Got a stomach like a rock.
Sonja:	Why do you want me to look at you? Why?

Man:	Because. You're beautiful. You musta been told that before.
Sonja:	Beautiful. What do you mean by beautiful?
Man:	Like a magazine cover, you know, so nice and slim, not like that bag my ex-wife, all that long blonde hair, and those long dancer's legs ya got, perfect, and and the joyful bosom there, and and—
Sonja:	My body will sag and die like everyone else's. I'll get fat when I'm forty, it runs in my family, my joyful bosom will probably fill with cancer, varicose veins will cover my legs and my knees and hips will have to be replaced. And I'll get cataracts over these crazy eyes. Then will I be beautiful?
Man:	Come on, let's go into the bush. Now.
Sonja:	What do you want from me?
Man:	I want to devour you.

He laughs, and kisses her, growling like a dog. She struggles to get away. She is breathless when she speaks.

Sonja:	Listen to me. Please, just listen to me and then kill me if you must. Just ask yourself what it is you really want from me. Really. What do you want?
Man:	When you're on fire, you jump in the water, babe. You don't stop to ask questions.
Sonja:	I am talking to you. Talk to me, I'm a person.

He takes a long knife from his pocket. She gasps.

Sonja:	What's that?
Man:	Just my hunting knife.
Sonja:	Let me go.
Man:	You come into this ravine lookin' for me. You been lookin' for me all your life.
Sonja:	I came looking for wilderness.
Man:	And what did you find?

Sonja: A predator. Stay away from me.

Man: I want you.

Sonja: No, you don't.

Man: I'm going to have you.

Sonja: You'll never have me. You can tear my body apart with your knife but you'll never reach me.

Man: Your eyes drives me wild, I think about your eyes and I toll like the bell.

Sonja: You want my eyes?

Man: I want your eyes to stroke me, stroke me with your eyes, come on, baby.

Sonja: You want my eyes?

Man: Oooh look at your face, fightin' face, blood red with anger, how come you're so mad, eh pretty? How come you're so mad?

Sonja: Because I'm tired of it. I hate it. I HATE IT! Ever since I was ten years old the men have been staring at me, wanting to devour me, all because I have blonde hair and a big bust. I couldn't walk down the street. Even down the aisle at church. In school, boys would whisper when I passed, and when they talked to me it was the way a wolf might talk to a rabbit, always with the devouring on their minds, always, always. I hate your desire.

Man: You liar. All you girls, you love gettin' looked at. Even my four-year-old, you should see her, preening in the mirror.

Sonja: I hate you. I HATE you.

Man: I love it when those sexy eyes of yours flash. I'd love those eyes to flash on my secret parts.

She takes the knife.

Man: Whatcha doin' with that knife? Give it back to me right now. Ooooh I like a wild girl. Come on, honey, give it here.

She cuts out her left eye.

Man: Holy Christ in heaven. Whatcha doin', man? You crazy witch. Hey! Hellllp!

Sonja: You want my eye? Here is my eye. Take it! Take it!

Man: Ahhhh. Stop that, come on. Stop it. Christ. This . . . this . . . isn't what I meant. (*He shouts out*) Hellllp.

Sonja: Yes it is. It is what you meant.

Man: You're a freak. Look at ya, blood drippin' all over you. You're crazy.

Sonja: And now I will cut off my hand, and then it will touch you anytime you want. Anywhere you want. All your secret parts.

Man: No! Please!

Sonja: There. Now you have my eye to look at you and my hand to touch you. Would you like my lips? To kiss you, to whisper in your ear?

Man: You keep away from me, freak. Get these things offa me, why are they stickin' to me? Get them offa me.

The man runs away, screaming, with her eye and hand and lip sticking to him. The woman kneels down.

Sonja: Oh, my good God in heaven, forgive me. Why did I give in to my rage, why did I do this? How will I watch over my children in the playground with only one eye, or see all their sweet heads on their pillows, how will I feed them and dress them with one hand, and how will I sing to them or whisper my love with no mouth? Oh! God forgive me.

And she lay down on the wet grass and fell unconscious from loss of blood. A group of teenagers who were heading down for a drinking party spotted her, and horrified by her disfigurement, covered her with their coats and sent the fastest runner in their group to call for help.

The ambulance attendants found her hand and her eye and her lip strewn along the path and brought them to the hospital where the surgeons sewed them back on.

The man told the story of the "crazy" woman he met in the ravine at different Toronto bars every night. It was the only time in his life people had been fascinated by him, and looked at him while he talked. He felt a warm flush through his body; he felt like a star. After he told his story, the listeners would shake their heads and ask him why a woman would do something like that.

"I really don't know," he would say, very quietly. And everybody looked at the floor. And before he left the bar, he always lowered his voice and said: "And this was a really pretty woman, right? Like, she was your fantasy girl."

But when he walked up Yonge Street he no longer stared at the young, heavily made-up girls leaning against the storefronts; for every time he looked, even by accident, at a girl, his eyeball would burn, and his hand would become infected and painful, and his mouth would fill with canker sores. Unfortunately, fear and pain were the only things that stopped him looking, for he still did not see anything wrong with the way he looked at the girls.

The woman lived with physical pain and discomfort for the rest of her life, but she lived in peace, because no man ever looked at her again with devouring eyes.

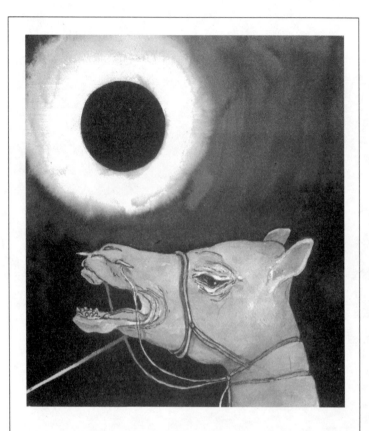

THE CAMEL WHO CRIED
IN THE SUN

RETOLD BY GRIFFIN ONDAATJE

THERE WAS A CAMEL WHO WALKED back and forth across the desert for about forty years, working for a man who never gave it enough food or water. And though it had worked its whole life for this one man it had never complained once to him. It kept quiet and walked across the desert carrying all sorts of goods from one city to another.

On each journey the camel carried seven large bundles, including pots and pans, flour, rice and water. And its owner would ride on top of all these bundles, guiding the camel on their journey towards whatever city they were destined for. The camel worked hard: it climbed steep sand dunes and walked along the tops of them and then lumbered down their other side, exhausted, almost tumbling over and spilling everything on a number of occasions. On the flat stretches of the desert the man always yelled at the camel to run. And even when it was too tired to do so, the camel would pick up a little speed, its long legs swinging out to its sides as if tripping over something and starting to fall.

But it never fell. And it rarely stopped to rest. The camel's whole life was spent staggering up and down sand dunes, and it seemed as if it were climbing across an ocean of sand, waves of sand rising a hundred feet high. And it continued on for years, arriving at each destination with dry and stinging eyes and with foam gathered around its mouth, sputtering and spitting on the ground as it breathed in and out noisily. It would stand and wait patiently in the sun while its owner climbed off its back and walked over to the shade to sit and talk business with clients.

One day, however, after years of hard work and walking in the burning sun and staggering over the desert's sandy waves, the camel felt water coming out of its eyes.

At first it didn't know what was happening. The camel thought that perhaps it was dying. But these were tears coming out of its eyes and they were joined by long, heaving sobs. The owner thought that the old camel was choking and he jumped off its back and stood a few yards away to give it enough room to spit out whatever it was choking on. Then he realized that it was only *crying*.

But it has never cried before, the owner thought to himself. He stood there speechless, as if watching a miracle—as if a fountain were rising out of the sand in front of him. Through its tears the camel could see its owner staring at it in disbelief and anger, and it looked at him apologetically—but continued crying. The camel cried for several minutes until the owner finally slapped its face and shouted at it to stop.

Later on in the evening, though, when its insensitive owner had fallen asleep, the camel cried alone under the huge desert sky. It cried softly and bit its lip and looked up at the quiet stars. It was feeling lonely now, because it was thinking about its long life of suffering and hard work.

And so, for the next few months, almost anything would set the camel crying. If the wind blew sand into its eyes it cried. Sometimes the camel stopped and stared at the ground sadly as its owner yelled and screamed at it to get moving again.

"Cry *one* more time . . . and I won't give you a drop of water!" the owner yelled.

And so, with restraint, the old camel never again cried in front of its owner. It would wait until nightfall, when its owner was fast asleep. The minute the owner finished eating and had fallen asleep, the camel would drift away like a boat, the bundles still tied to its back, and sink behind a sand dune, and cry until morning. As for the owner, he couldn't hear the camel crying. He would sleep soundly at nights, and during the days he'd ride on the camel's back and it was as if he were floating over the desert on a bundle of valuable goods under which there was no camel.

One day they approached the city of Medina.

It was the middle of a hot day of walking and climbing, and the owner was growing very sleepy. The camel was walking slower and slower since the air was unbelievably hot and difficult to breathe. The sun didn't seem to move but stayed for hours in the middle of the sky. The man was drowsy, sitting high up on those bundles, rocking back and forth with the motion of the camel. He could barely keep his eyes open, and his back ached. When they reached the foot of a large sand dune he yelled at the camel to climb faster.

They reached the top of the sand dune and he ordered the camel to stop. The camel was wheezing and craning its neck towards the ground, foam dripping from its mouth. It gasped for breath. The owner ignored the camel and looked far across the desert to the north where he could see the outskirts of Medina in the distance. It was only a few miles away.

"Sleepy . . . ," he said to himself, leaning over. He crawled down the side of the camel and half-fell onto the sand. "Don't move while I rest," he said. Then he lay down in the shade of the camel, made a pillow of sand with a wide sweep of his arm and fell asleep.

So the camel stood still with the seven bundles on its back.

Hours passed and the camel still stood patiently on the hot sand. It moved only when the sun moved, in order to keep a cool blanket of shadow covering its owner. Standing in the hot sun for hours, the camel couldn't help itself and it started to moan a little. As usual, the owner didn't hear a thing—he was in a deep sleep, dreaming about arriving in Medina.

The six or seven bundles felt terribly heavy to the camel. Its feet burned in the sand and its legs began to ache. The camel finally looked towards Medina and cried quietly. Soon its whole body began to shake—the way animals shake when they cry in secret. Tears filled its eyes and as it stared down at the ground it watched them fall, without a sound, into the sand.

But then, suddenly, the camel stopped crying. It sniffed the air and blinked. It saw something in the distance. Though its eyes were watery and it couldn't see far, it saw what looked like a white flame wavering on the desert. Soon the camel could see that it was a man walking up the sand dune.

The Prophet lived in Medina, and it was he who came walking up this hill . . . and when he reached the top of the hill he walked straight up and hugged the surprised camel's neck, pressing his face against its long bony face. He stared into the camel's black eyes and then offered his shoulder for support. And with a sigh of relief the camel leaned down heavily on his shoulder, and immediately it burst into tears, letting out long sobs of unhappiness.

And then something miraculous happened: the tears that fell from the camel's eyes dropped into the sand and sank down, filtering magically into the sleeping owner's dream.

And the owner began to dream that he saw everything through the camel's eyes. He saw how the Prophet walked up the hill, and held the camel while it cried.

Dreaming there, in the shade of the camel and the Prophet, the owner felt his heart ache with sadness. He saw for the first time the terrible condition the camel was in and he felt, as the camel felt, a lifetime of pain and loneliness. He lay there and wept in his dream, into his pillow of sand, while the camel cried against the shoulder of the Prophet.

When the camel had finally finished crying, the Prophet stood back and looked down at the sleeping man who was still crying.

"Are you the camel's owner?" he asked.

"Messenger of God, I . . . ," answered the sleeping man from where he lay in the sand. He was about to speak when a wave of sadness came over him and he lost his voice and was unable to say anything else.

"Why can't you hear it crying?" continued the Prophet.

Though the man tried to answer, the Prophet didn't stay to hear him. The Prophet turned and walked away down the hill, back towards Medina.

An hour later, as the owner finally began to surface from his dream he felt his face grow hotter and hotter. He was feverish, dreaming that the sun's flames, as sharp as pineapple leaves, were falling onto his face.

He sat up then, eyes wide, awake from his dream. He couldn't remember anything he had dreamed about. Yet he noticed that the camel was standing half-way down the hill, staring out towards the city. The sun had moved across the sky and was now touching the horizon.

The man got to his feet slowly. He could feel on his face that he'd been crying and for an instant he recalled that the camel had been in his dream. Then he walked down the hill and stood peacefully beside the old camel, and the two of them stared out across the desert towards Medina.

HOW THE GODS AND DEMONS
LEARNED TO PLAY TOGETHER

RETOLD BY ERNEST MACINTYRE

THE GREAT GOD OF THE HINDUS is Lord Brahma and in ancient times the great book of the Hindus made up of many parts was called the Vedas. Like the Bible of the Christians and the Koran of the Islamic people the Vedas told the Hindus how to lead good and proper lives. India is a very large place. In those ancient days there was no office like the United Nations in New York where all the countries of the world had a large map of many colours showing where one country ended and another began. People just moved across the land from one place to another, meeting other, different kinds of people as they went. Lord Brahma and his Hindus who started in the north of India began moving to the south, carrying with them the great books of the Vedas. The people of Lord Brahma moved right across the whole of southern India and into the country now called Sri Lanka, for in those days the narrow and shallow sea that divides Sri Lanka from India was all land.

In all these southern parts that the Hindus had come to there lived a great many tribes who behaved in different ways from the Hindus. The tribes of the southern lands, in their own way, lived like the Aboriginal people of Australia, hunting, and gathering fruits. We know today that it is wrong to say that the Egyptian people who built the great pyramids or the Sri Lankan people who built the wonderful tanks and temples of Anuradhapura or the Tamil Nadu people who danced the beautiful Bharata Natyam were superior or better or more civilized than the Aboriginal people of Australia. They were not because we know today that civilized means to live happily with whatever you have in the land around you. In that way the Aboriginal people of Australia and the tribal people of South India were as civilized as the people of Lord Brahma, the Hindus. But the Hindus did not see it that way. The Hindus thought that they were more civilized, superior to the tribal people of the south. As the English thought that they were superior when they first came to Australia, as the French and English thought when they first arrived in North America.

And this story of ours began because the Hindus thought that they were better than the tribal people of the south.

God Indra, who worked under Lord Brahma, had been worried and angry for some time about strange noises coming from the direction of the forests where the tribal people of the southern lands lived. Not long after the sun had set he would hear, quite distinctly, long and piercing shrieks, the beating of drums, wailing, chanting and the stamping of feet. One night he decided to see for himself. Moving up silently to a large bush behind which he could hide, he peered through its leaves at the forest clearing beyond, and saw the tribal people behaving in a way that he had never seen before. There was a woman seated on the ground looking very ill. About ten yards in front of her there were two pillars made of the trunks of banana trees and a third banana trunk was fixed to the top of the other two so that it looked like a kind of doorway. On both sides and on top of this doorway were tied great bundles of jungle leaves and branches so that you couldn't see what was behind the door. All the tribal people had come there and were standing on either side of the sick woman as well as behind her, but all of them were looking at the doorway made of banana trunks and jungle branches. Between the woman and the doorway two men were leaping into the air as they danced with large flaming torches held in their hands. Another man sat close to the doorway beating a drum for the dancers. A fourth man, dressed in jungle leaves like all the others, moved about near the doorway shouting and singing something that Indra couldn't understand. And then, all of a sudden, as this man shouted very loud, and the drum was beaten louder than ever and the dancers leapt in the air higher than ever, a terrible shriek was heard from behind the doorway. Everyone stopped doing what they were doing. In the silence the shriek was heard again and through the door there leapt a huge and terrible looking demon with the head of a bear and the body of a human being. The man who had been chanting and singing shouted "Mahasona! Mahasona!" and hearing this Indra knew that the name of the demon was Mahasona. Immediately the singing man asked the demon Mahasona:

"What do you want to make this woman well again?"

Mahasona replied, "I want a baby human to take away, and I will make this woman well again."

"No! No! A baby human cannot be given to you," said the singing man, with great feeling.

"Then what will you give?" asked the demon Mahasona.

"I can give you a small chicken that is already dead," said the man.

"Then give me the small chicken that is already dead," agreed Mahasona the demon.

The singing man then walked up to a small basket lying on the ground close to where the people were standing. From the basket he took up a little dead chicken. But as he held it up to show Mahasona the demon, Indra struck. Indra had been getting angrier and angrier as he watched these things that the tribal people were doing. Being a god of the Hindus, he thought that these things were evil and uncivilized. Indra rushed forward with his famous staff. Indra always carried a tall staff and he used it on his enemies. He attacked the demon Mahasona who then ran back through the door to enter the jungle again. All the people and dancers started screaming and running in all directions. Inside the jungle Indra caught up with the demon Mahasona and gave him such a beating that he fell to the ground, screaming. But Indra did not stop there. That night he went full speed through the whole jungle attacking and beating all the demons with his staff, hundreds of them. By morning all the demons had been well beaten and Indra's victory over the demons became famous with all the Hindu gods and with the Lord of all gods, Brahma.

The next morning after Lord Brahma had eaten his breakfast of bananas, curds and honey washed down with milk from a brass goblet, he called up Indra to say thank you for his great defeat of the demons of the southern tribal lands. But the moment he saw Indra he knew that Indra was not fully happy with what had happened. Indra had a thoughtful look on his face. Brahma asked him, "What is the matter?"

Indra, speaking slowly, said, "We will never be able to live with these people happily simply by defeating their demons, because their demons belong to them. We must win the hearts and minds of the tribal people and their demons."

"Yes, I know that," said Brahma.

"But how do we win their hearts and minds?" asked Indra.

Brahma gave a deep sigh, waited a moment and then spoke:

"Ah, if only they could listen to our great Vedas. If they listened to our holy books they would surely give up their evil ways." Brahma sighed again: "But these are low-caste people, born as Sudras, and you know that Sudras are not allowed to listen to the Vedas. The Vedas can never be listened to by low-caste people."

Because Brahma spoke slowly Indra had time to think while he was listening, and suddenly he got an idea from what Brahma was saying. Indra was very excited.

"Yes, Lord Brahma, but that rule is only for the Vedas that we now have!"

Brahma looked curiously at Indra. "So what do you mean?"

Indra spoke quickly. "If we make another, new Veda especially for the uncivilized low-castes, then they can learn our good ways from this new Veda! They are not allowed to listen only to the first great Vedas. They can listen to a new one."

Brahma turned his head to look more closely at Indra. It looked as if Indra was right, for Brahma said a slow "Hmmm." And then he asked, "But how do we do this? You see, Indra, we must know more about these low castes before we can make a new Veda for them. Now tell me, last night when you watched them from behind the bush, what were they doing?"

Indra then told Brahma all about the sick woman, the crowds around her looking at the doorway of banana trunks and jungle branches, the dancing men with torches in their hands, the music of the drum, the singing of the man who offered a little dead chicken to the demon Mahasona, the shrieking demon and how it suddenly entered from behind the door. Brahma then thought for a long time about what Indra had described to him, keeping his head up to the sky, using his left hand to hold his chin. The fingers of his right hand kept tapping on his big stomach, now full of curds, honey and bananas. Finally he turned his head back to Indra with a very knowing look in the small eyes inside his pudgy face. He spoke:

"So you say that these uncivilized, low-caste Sudras can actually sing?"

Indra nodded.

"You also saw them dancing?"

Indra nodded again.

"And they made music with the drum?"

"Oh yes!" said Indra.

"Hmmm—and from what you have told me I can see that these people have feelings, like our Hindu people."

"Very much more, I think," Indra said. "They don't think carefully like us, they show too much feeling. I saw it last night from behind the bushes."

Brahma now rose very slowly, and stood a little while longer in silence and then said, "I think I have an idea." He thought a little again and said, "And you say that the sick woman and the people watching all this were on one side and the dancing men, the singing man, the drummer and the demon Mahasona were on the other side?"

"Something like that," said Indra.

Brahma went on, "And the demon entered from the door on his side?"

"Yes," said Indra, wondering why Brahma was so interested in the way things had happened that night.

After another long silence, Brahma said, "Come and see me tomorrow at this same time."

As Indra bowed and went away Brahma sat down again. But now he crossed his legs in a special way and folded his arms over his chest also in a special way, which helped him to think very, very deeply. The Hindus call this Yoga. He remained like this for many, many hours.

When Indra went the next morning Brahma was standing up, waiting for him. As soon as he saw Indra he said, "I have done it!"

"What?" asked Indra as his eye fell on a large book in Brahma's right hand.

"I have made a new Veda from which the low castes can learn our good ways," said Brahma waving the big book.

Brahma and Indra then excitedly spoke these lines:

Indra: Tell me about it.

Brahma: They will learn things, not by listening to the new Veda as we did with the old Vedas, but by playing with the help of the new Veda.

Indra: By playing?

Brahma: Yes, the new Veda tells them how to play, and when they play people will learn wise and good things.

Indra: What is the meaning of *to play?*

Brahma: To play is to pretend, to imitate.

Indra: How do they pretend?

Brahma: They will play or pretend in a way that they are already used to.

Indra: What is that?

Brahma: Like what you saw that night when you were hiding behind the bushes. That is why I wanted you to tell me what they were doing that night. You see, Indra, they are used to having people on one side of the ground watching something going on on the other side with dancing, music, singing, chanting and speaking.

Indra: Yes.

Brahma: What you saw that night was real, but my new Veda is going to use the same way of doing things for playing or pretending.

Indra: What will they pretend or play? I hope it will not be the things I saw that night. Even pretending those things will be terrible.

Brahma: Ah no, it won't be those things.

Indra: Then what?

Brahma: What they will pretend and play are the stories from the *Mahabharata* and the *Ramayana* and otherwise, and good books of us Hindus. And they will be happy to play these stories because they already know a little of how to play.

Indra: They already know how to play?

Brahma: Sometimes you don't listen to me carefully enough. I told you a moment ago that what you saw that night was real but I am going to ask them to do it the same way for

	playing the stories of the *Mahabharata* and the *Ramayana*.
Indra:	Is that the new Veda in your hand?
Brahma:	Yes.
Indra:	May I please look at it, Lord Brahma?
Brahma:	Yes, in a moment.
Indra:	Why is the book so big, Lord Brahma?
Brahma:	Because there is a lot in it for dancers to learn, for musicians to learn, for actors to learn.
Indra:	Actors?
Brahma:	Yes, because when they play these stories they will only pretend or act as if they are real, they will be called actors.

And so the first book in the world about how to make a play was given by Lord Brahma to Indra about two thousand years ago. It was called the *Natyasastra*. "Natya" means play and "sastra" means the art, in the ancient Sanskrit language of the Hindus.

Now Indra had the book in his hand and Brahma could see that he was very excited by the way he thanked Brahma.

"Oh, Lord Brahma, thank you for the *Natyasastra*. Now the low castes, the Sudras, have a way of learning our good ways, just by playing."

But Lord Brahma had some advice for Indra when he said:

"But the *Natyasastra* can be used by everybody. And now you have work to do, because I have given you only the book on how to do a play. You will now have to go and do a play to see how it works. *So go now and do the first play in the world for all to see.*"

Indra hesitated, asking, "But what shall this world's first play be about?"

"Ah! I have thought about that too," said Brahma. "Because all this began when you peeped through the bushes, saw their ways and attacked the demon Mahasona and all the other demons that night, let the world's first play be about Indra's defeat of the demons!"

Indra was very pleased. He got the help of a famous wise and learned old Hindu by the name of Bharata Muni to select actors, train them and do the play. So the day of the world's first play came and it was performed at a big open place on a moonlit night.

But when the play began, a very strange thing happened. All the demons who had been beaten by Indra, except Mahasona, had got well again and were at the play. Mahasona, who was still very sore, remained at home. And only one of the other demons knew that Mahasona was not at the play. His name was Hiranya Kassipu. On the way to the play Kassipu had stopped at the home of Mahasona and seen him in bed. When the first scene of the play began, an actor dressed like Mahasona came shrieking in and an actor dressed like Indra rushed forward and pretended to beat the actor dressed like Mahasona. At this moment the hundreds of demons who had come to see the play got very angry and excited because they thought that the whole thing was real. They had looked around, and seeing that Mahasona was not with them in the audience, thought that it was the real Mahasona, their pal, who was being beaten by the real Indra. They thought that the defeat of the demons was happening again, a second time! So all the demons except Kassipu rushed forward and beat up the man playing Indra and smashed up the whole play.

Only Kassipu remained calm, seated on the grass. He knew it was not real. But strangely, though he knew it was a play, he felt very sad to see even an actor dressed like Mahasona being beaten up.

Indra, very upset that the world's first play had been smashed up, rushed to Lord Brahma that very night and asked what should be done. This time Brahma did not have to go deep in thought. The answer was very clear.

"Protect the actors," he said.

"How?" asked Indra.

"Build a house and do the plays inside, a playhouse, a theatre!" replied Brahma.

And so the world's first playhouse was built with four strong walls and a very safe roof. At one end on a raised platform the actors acted, coming in and going out through a door on the stage that led, at the back, to a resting room. At the other end of the room the people sat and watched the play.

But Indra and the other gods were still unhappy. By protecting the actors they were also keeping the demons and the low castes out of the theatre. So they all went to Lord Brahma and explained, "Oh, Lord Brahma, you gave us the *Natyasastra* and from it we have learned the art of acting and how to do a play. And you did all this in the first place to teach our good ways to the Sudras and their demons. But they are now being kept out of the theatre. We can see them hanging around suspiciously outside the walls, wondering what is going on inside. It is all very sad."

From the way Brahma looked at them they could see that he had been thinking in the same way.

"Yes," he said, "and that is why I have asked all the demons to meet me tonight. All of you must come. I have asked the wise old Bharata Muni who trained the actors to explain to the demons what a play is."

That night when all the gods and demons met, Bharata Muni began by saying, "You demons attacked the play last night because you thought it was real. Plays are not real, they are acted."

Immediately the demon Kassipu said, "But I knew that Mahasona did not come for the play. I knew that two people dressed up like Mahasona and Indra were acting, and yet I too felt sad to see the demons being defeated."

"So did you also attack the play as the other demons did?" asked Bharata Muni.

"No, I did not. I felt sad but did not do anything," said Kassipu.

"Ah! So you behaved differently from the other demons who thought it was real, and I will tell you why. Listen, O demons! It is because of you that people will always think that they feel real feelings whenever they see a play," exclaimed Bharata Muni.

"Why is that?" asked the demon Kassipu. "What have we got to do with it?"

"To make this new thing called a play, to make drama, Lord Brahma took something from you demons and something else from the gods," explained Bharata Muni.

Kassipu then asked, "What did Lord Brahma take from us?"

"Feelings," said Bharata Muni.

"How is that?" inquired Kassipu.

Bharata Muni had to explain carefully. "Lord Brahma heard from Indra about the woman who was ill that night. How the tribal people called you demons to make her well. How there was such a lot of feeling when you asked for a little takeaway baby but the people refused and offered you a dead takeaway chicken instead. Lord Brahma saw that the tribal people and their demons were full of feelings in a way that gods are not, and he knew that a play must have a lot of feeling and that will come from you, not from the gods."

"Then what have the gods given to this new thing called a play?" asked the demon Kassipu.

"They have given something as important as feelings," said Bharata Muni. "The gods have done something to stop people from letting their feelings make them think that these plays are real, and get excited, and do things such as you all did when you smashed up the world's first play."

"How did the gods do that?" inquired Kassipu.

"By beautiful music, beautiful songs, beautiful dances, beautiful words, all taken from their great books the Vedas," said Bharata Muni, smiling.

"I do not understand," Kassipu complained.

Bharata Muni explained again carefully. "You see, demons, in real life if I am going to kill someone I will not do a beautiful dance and do it. I will not sing a beautiful song and do it, I will not use beautiful words when I am doing it. And so, when I do it in this way in a play you will have strong feelings but will not get excited and get up and try to stop the actor from acting in a way as if he is killing the other actor. Do you understand?"

All the demons smiled and said together, "Yes, now we understand."

The next night they all got together and did another play, also about gods and demons and this time there was no disturbance. They knew that the great feeling in the play came from the demons and the beauty in the play came from the gods. They learned to play together.

THE GREAT JOURNEY

RETOLD BY LINDA SPALDING

PRINCE YUDHISTHIRA AND HIS FOUR younger brothers shared a king-dom in Northern India, reigning together without conflict even to the point that they loved and shared one wife. Their cousin was Krishna, who was known for his tenderness, laughter and wisdom, and the brothers looked to him for guidance. As a result, their kingdom was a happy place, where people devoted themselves to love.

But one afternoon, as the five brothers and their wife Draupadi were sitting on a terrace, eating moist raisin cake and drinking raisin wine, a messenger arrived and stood behind some bushes, waiting to be received. "It's always something," said Yudhisthira, the oldest brother. He was tired of public life and longed to retire to a mountain and live a spiritual life, but he'd made a vow to Krishna that he would always protect the helpless and give aid to the needy, so he stayed with his wife and brothers in order to do his share of worldly work.

"He looks so tired," Draupadi said, pitying the young messenger. "We shouldn't keep him out there waiting in the sun." Draupadi's voice was as soft as her heart. "I'll go and talk to him," she said to Yudhisthira, brushing some crumbs off his sleeve fondly. Then she hurried down the stone steps to the bushes that lined the gravel path. Unlike her husbands, Draupadi hadn't travelled in the mountain passes and valleys of the kingdom, and her only information about the outside world came from messengers who were usually frightened and exhausted boys overwhelmed by the palace and its royal brothers. "Come and have a piece of cake before you speak," she said warmly, clasping her hands in front of her in the gesture of greeting. But the young messenger shook his head. "I'm here because Lord Krishna is dying," he said, twisting a piece of his scarf in his hand.

Draupadi pulled him along the path, calling out sharply to her hus-bands, and even as she did this a cloud came between the palace and the sun, and birds who had been flickering in and out of the flowering trees began lifting away from the garden in alarm. When the five brothers heard the terrible news, they drew their robes around them-selves tightly and sat looking out at the land that surrounded them. Yudhisthira wiped at his face with the back of his hand and said he didn't want to be a prince without his cousin's help. He was tired of the world. Tired of responsibilities. "I'm going into the mountains," Yudhisthira said. Then he said, "No. I'm going even farther, all the way to the other world. I'm finished with this one."

His brothers looked out at everything they had known and created, although the terrace was dark now and there was a terrible silence in the garden that they couldn't understand. "We're coming with you," they said. "You won't be alone."

Draupadi went inside and gathered up all the beautiful linens and silks the five brothers had always worn. Someone will enjoy these, she thought, pausing over a favourite shirt of Yudhisthira's and rubbing it against her face. She thought then that she would never smell this beloved husband or touch him again unless she accompanied him to the other world. Tucking some dried flowers and cinnamon sticks around the soft shirts and trousers and robes of the other brothers, she unwrapped her own sash, which had been embroidered by her grandmother, and gave it to her maid. She took off her bracelets and the necklace that was the sign of her married status and left them under the pillow on her bed. Then she unwrapped her sari, which was made of many yards of the finest silk, and folded it and packed it with all her other silks and brocades and sent them all into the village where other women would enjoy them.

That night, when the shutters of the capital city were closed against intruders, the six travellers left the palace and went quietly to the gates of the city. They had no bags and carried no food and because of their simple cotton clothes the gatekeeper took them for sadhus and wished them a safe journey. Just outside the gates, a thin dog came up to them, circling restlessly. His head was tilted as if his neck had been broken and his tongue hung out of the side of his mouth. "He's rabid," one of the brothers said, and Bhima, the youngest, picked up a stick. But Draupadi admonished him. "Since we're going to the other world anyway," she said, "let the poor thing come along."

Bhima fell to the back of the line then, and the dog began circling the group, running in longer and longer strides with his strange tilt until he had herded them away from the gates of their kingdom and off to the road that led to the east. Yudhisthira was sure that Mount Meru, with heaven at its peak, lay to the north of them, but Draupadi said, "I've never travelled at all. Let's journey together for a while," and he couldn't deny her that last pleasure.

In a day or two of walking into the rising sun, the companions reached the edge of a desert, where there were a few tents set up against the sand and some travellers who invited them to eat. "Come," they insisted. "Sit down and eat and drink and tell us about your pilgrimage. You must be sadhus, aren't you?"

The next day and the next and the next, the brothers and their wife and the circling dog walked many miles, skirting the edge of the desert, taking whatever food was offered, until they smelled the thick, briny smell of an ocean ahead of them. "Let's turn north please," Yudhisthira suggested, because he was longing to be done with the journey. "We're all exhausted with this life." He stopped under a tall ficus tree and leaned against it but the dog took Yudhisthira's sleeve in his teeth and the second oldest brother said, "Look, I've always been able to figure things out, and I've never been proved wrong. I say we are too smart to give up this world without testing it to the fullest. I say we should feel the ocean spray on our hot, dry skin before we give up this world. Listen, I can hear its thunder from here; it can't be far. I say, we should go on and I am always right, aren't I?"

Bhima said, "I've got plenty of strength left, that's for sure. I could carry all of you if you're too tired to carry yourselves!"

The dog let go of Yudhisthira's sleeve and began circling the tired group, edging them along the road towards the huge ocean, with its rolling waves, its breakers with foam as white as snow, and its great gulls who flew above them looking for fish. The dog ran ahead when he saw the gulls, barking excitedly, and then at the shore they all turned south because the dog ran along chasing the gulls. The dog loved to chase birds and it was not yet ready to give up this activity.

In a village people welcomed the travellers and gave them food. In this way the five brothers and their wife and the dog journeyed to the tip of India until they could look across the channel to the beautiful land of Sri Lanka.

But they headed west and north, then, because Yudhisthira insisted that it was time to find Mount Meru and, because they loved him, the brothers finally agreed and the dog kept pace and helped them find enough food and shelter to keep up their journey.

As they walked, Yudhisthira meditated, trying to focus on the principles of yoga, which told him to give up the desires of this world, to loosen the knots of attachments that bound him to life. He thought of Krishna and longed to follow his example and, without speaking further, he led his loved ones up the sub-continent of India and through the Himalayas until they came to the great desert that they had skirted before. The sand of this desert was so hot that it burned their feet through the thin leather of their sandals and a stinging wind hit their hands and faces until they covered everything but their eyes with the shreds of cotton they had worn for weeks, and even then sand blew through the gauze and clung to their eyelashes and lips. There was no plant alive in that desert, no water, and no food. At night the sun disappeared and the sand lost its warmth and there was nothing to do but huddle around the dog, who lay against them and licked their faces and eyes. "Thank heaven for this creature," Draupadi said one morning, trying to sit up and reaching weakly to stroke the coarse fur on his back. She touched the small, pointed bone between its ears and rubbed the twisted neck and drew some comfort from the dog, who lay beside her quietly. "I can't go much further," Draupadi said. Then she lay back with a long sigh and closed her eyes and the brothers, who adored her and who had known her all her life, rubbed her hands and feet and urged her to get up while it was still cool enough to travel.

The sun rose and Draupadi lifted her hand but she stopped breathing and they saw that she would never get up again.

"Our wife is dead," Bhima said. And because he was the strongest of the five, he wept loudest. "But why has this happened to her when she never hurt anyone or anything as long as she lived?"

Yudhisthira shook his head miserably. He was sitting next to the body of his wife but he stood up and wiped his eyes, which were running with tears. "Perhaps she favoured one of us over another," he said softly. Then he told his brothers that they would wait until nightfall and walk when the wind was cold instead of hot, and when the moon rose, they would go on, speaking no more about Draupadi.

That night the brothers and the dog walked on, but after a few hours two of the brothers lay down, just as Draupadi had done, and died within minutes on the dark sand. The next night another brother fell. Each of them had slumped to the ground without warning while Yudhisthira walked on, meditating on detachment and trying to release himself from the ties of this world.

"Why did they fall?" Bhima demanded. "Stop and talk to me, brother."

Yudhisthira turned and the dog stopped circling and came and sat at his feet. "I think our second brother was a little proud of his wisdom," Yudhisthira answered. "And our third brother was so good looking. He took such good care of himself and enjoyed so much the eyes of others. And our fourth brother was so strong. He liked to use his strength, do you remember?"

Bhima could hardly bring himself to listen. The thought that he'd left his wife and three of his brothers behind in the desert was unbearable to him, but he stumbled along after Yudhisthira, who walked calmly ahead, never once looking back. Suddenly Bhima cried out, "Oh God, brother, I'm dying; I know I am; I'm going to fall in this godforsaken desert like the others."

Yudhisthira stopped and the dog whined sadly. "Why am I dying," Bhima cried again, sinking to his knees, "even before I reach Mount Meru? It isn't fair! I want to see it with my human eyes."

"Perhaps you are too greedy, my brother," Yudhisthira said. "You are wanting with all your strength." And without looking back again, he continued on his journey with the dog as his only companion.

At the edge of the sand the mountain rose like a mirage, a perfect cone, its snow-capped peak circled by a ring of cloud. Yudhisthira looked up at it, remembering to untie the knots that bound him to the world he had loved for so long, loosening his knees and hips in their sockets, unflexing his hands, blinking his eyes and opening his mouth so that it filled with a thousand pieces of warm air. He tried to close his ears but that was impossible and above him he heard the sharp cry of birds as if all the birds of his ancient, lost kingdom had found him— the birds who had deserted him like his strength when Krishna died. Looking up, he saw them assemble overhead and take on the shape of the god Indra. "Lift your arms so I can pull you," said the shape. But Yudhisthira covered his eyes and shook his head. "How can I go with you," he answered, "and leave my wife and brothers lying in the desert. Take them too and I'll be glad to go, but I can't go alone."

"Your brothers and Draupadi are waiting on Mount Meru," said the god. "They shed their bodies, but you may go to them as you are, both body and spirit intact."

Yudhisthira realized that he hadn't felt joy of any kind for months. Now he smiled but he said, "And this dog? He's been with us through everything in all our travels. He came to us when we set out from our capital and he never left us for a minute, even when there was nothing to eat or drink and when the sand stung his eyes and filled his ears and mouth. I can't abandon him to this horrible desert after all that."

"It's not possible for a dog to enter heaven," said Indra. "A dog is unclean. A dog has no soul. You must leave the dog here."

"I made a vow," Yudhisthira muttered to himself. "And even if I hadn't, it's worse to forsake a friend or refuse to help someone in need than anything else in the world. It's worse to forsake a friend than to murder a Brahmin." To Indra he said, "I made a vow once that I would never refuse help to anyone and I can't go against it even for the sake of eternal bliss."

"You're a great one to talk about vows," said Indra, "after you abandoned your wife and brothers! After you left them lying in the desert and pushed on for your own sake."

"I left them lying on the ground," replied Yudhisthira, "because I could do nothing for them. They had died, and no one can help the dead." While he spoke, he leaned down to the dog and stroked the bony part of its skull between its ears. The dog's long, pink tongue hung out of the side of its mouth. It stopped circling and stood still, but as Yudhisthira stroked its head it began to grow shorter in the face and neck and wider at the shoulders. It leaned back and lifted its paws and opened its mouth and began to howl and in the sound of the howl the god Indra could discern a few sounds that made sense to him, sounds that told him the dog was pleased with Yudhisthira's devotion and glad to be the companion of a man who would give up eternity rather than be false to his friend. Yudhisthira listened, too, and in the sound of the howl he discerned the wise voice of Dharma. "Even when I came to you as a dog," Dharma howled, "you called me a friend."

Yudhisthira laughed and he held the dog's paws up to his own chest and the two creatures began to move as if they were dancing at the edge of the great desert and at the foot of the great mountain and before they stopped dancing both of them were surrounded by the flock of birds and lifted up, by paws and arms, to the top of Mount Meru, where they received all the wisdom and strength and beauty and peace and solitude and companionship they could ever have desired.

Their two hearts were full then. They were radiant.

FATE AND FORTUNE

RETOLD BY GRAEME MACQUEEN

ONCE UPON A TIME there was a king of Benares named Fortune. The sun, the rain and the wind smiled on his land, and his people were fat and innocent. When he was young Fortune learned how to take his share of his people's wealth, and he grew rich. When he was older he learned how to take more than his share, and he grew very rich. His treasury bulged, his storehouse bulged and his granary bulged. As for his army, it would take me more time than I have to describe its magnificence.

In the neighbouring kingdom of Kosala lived a king named Fate. The sun, the rain and the wind frowned on his land. For half the year his people waded up to their waists in water and for half the year they watched the sun bake their land like a brick. Their food was thin *dal* with neither salt nor spices. Fate and his Queen shared the general poverty without complaint, and they named their treasury the Void, their storehouse the Vacant Lot and their granary the Echo Chamber. Of their pitiful army, the less that is said the better.

Now Fortune sent out spies to discover the condition of the kingdom of Kosala, and when they returned they made their report.

"Poor, Your Majesty, is the realm of Kosala. Like a dry stick, Lord, is this kingdom, ready to be snapped."

"But what of Fate's treasury, his storehouse and granary? What of his army?"

"His treasury, Majesty, is called The Void, his storehouse is called The Vacant Lot and his granary is called The Echo Chamber. Of his pitiful army, the less that is said the better."

"This being the case," said Fortune to his counsellors, "why not take Kosala?"

"Indeed, Your Majesty, why not?"

So Fortune had his Fourfold Army prepared, and infantry, cavalry, chariots and elephants began to mass on the border of Kosala.

Word of the preparations reached Fate, and he was forced to consider his situation. "Kosala is like a dry stick," he thought, "and if we resist we will be broken in a single snap. Many people will be killed. Would it not be better if I simply renounced the throne? Then Fortune could march in and take what he wanted without causing misery."

So Fate and the Queen left quietly in darkness disguised as ascetics, their features smeared with dirt and their clothes the meanest rags. They followed cowpaths and ill-favoured roads.

Fortune marched into Kosala. There was little to take, but what there was he took without hesitation. Fate and the Queen made their way to an outlying part of Benares, just inside the city walls, knowing that the King's spies would not think to look in his chief city. They took up their dwelling in an open space next to a potter's shed, begging their daily food and passing the time in meditation and in each other's company.

By and by the Queen became pregnant, and in due course she gave birth to a son, whom they named Fair. He was a sweet and gentle child, and he played with the children from the neighbourhood. But when he reached adolescence Fate said to the Queen, "Lady, it is time for our son to be educated, and to be trained in all arts and crafts. He may have need of such learning. Moreover, the King of Benares has never stopped searching for us, and if he finds us he will kill the lad as well. Let us send our son outside the walls of Benares." And the Queen agreed. So Fair left home and trained in all the branches of learning and in all arts and crafts. He learned about sacred and obscure texts, he learned how to ride a horse and use a sword, he learned how to make fine speeches, he learned how to sing and to play the lute. In short, he became an accomplished young man.

Now Fortune had a personal attendant, barber and gossip-monger who had formerly served Fate. He was low-down and mean-spirited, and he had developed the habit of turning his head continually from side to side, always attempting to spy out Fate and his wife, for he knew betraying them would win him a fortune. One day he was employed on some business or other in a poor section of Benares and was hurrying past a potter's shed trying to avoid stepping in anything foul when he turned his head to the left and saw an ascetic moving slowly and with great dignity, carrying a begging bowl. "Don't I know this fellow?" he thought. "No, it is impossible!" And he scurried on. Then he turned his head to the right and saw a female ascetic sitting on the earth, her hair in great dreadlocks, her face soiled, the rags falling from her body. As he watched she rose to her feet and walked, and she walked like a queen. In an instant he knew the truth, and he went straight to King Fortune and told him everything.

Summoning his men, and telling them to take the barber as their guide, Fortune gave them instructions to seize Fate and the Queen and to bring them to him. They did so. And when they were brought to him, the King of Benares said, without looking at his captives:

"Take them and tie their arms behind their backs with stout, strong cords. Tie their arms as tightly as a thing can be tied. Shave their heads with a razor and parade them through the streets to the harsh sound of the Panava drum. When they have been displayed in all the streets and crossroads take them out through the southern gate of the city and execute them in the usual manner."

Now, in the meantime Fair had been thinking, "It is a long time since I have seen my mother and father. How fine it would be to visit them." So he entered the gates of Benares with a crowd of pilgrims, intending to head directly for his home near the potter's shed. But he heard, in the distance, the harsh sound of the Panava drum, and he saw a crowd of people gathered beside the main thoroughfare. Drawing near, he saw that a man and a woman were being taken along the street by an armed guard of the King. They were clothed in rags and their heads were shaved. "How tightly their arms are bound," he thought. "How it must hurt them!" Then they raised their heads and he saw their faces, and they were his own mother and father.

Fair felt his limbs grow weak and his senses dim. Then he saw the royal guards, with their splendid uniforms and gleaming weapons, abusing his parents, and a new and awful feeling came upon him. It was the poison of hatred.

Following the crowd, he watched as his mother and father were displayed throughout Benares. But at the crossroad nearest the southern gate his father looked out over the crowd and saw him. And raising his voice loudly he cried out: "Fair! Fair!" The guards, not knowing he was addressing his son, mocked him, saying: "Are you asking for fair weather for your execution? Cheer up, the weather is always fair in Benares." But Fate, closing his eyes, spoke loudly and clearly:

"Dear One, beware
the poison of hatred.
Hatred ends not by hatred.

Dear One, beware.
For hatred ends
Only by letting it go."

Three times Fate spoke these words, and the guards laughed at him and said he was mad. But Fair heard and knew the words were meant for him.

Then the soldiers took Fate and the Queen outside the southern gate and executed them as they had been ordered, reporting all this to the King and leaving behind a few men to watch over the bodies. And Fair bought liquor in the city, offered it to the guards, and said in a loud, coarse voice, "Come then, let's drink to the death of the traitors from Kosala!" So the guards drank till they were rolling and groaning and puking on the ground, and Fair took wood and built a funeral pyre. Gathering his parents' bodies and placing them on the pyre, he lit the fire and walked around it three times, his palms joined in reverence. In short, he did what had to be done, according to the custom of the time and place, to honour his parents. But he felt neither pity nor love, for hatred had taken up residence in his heart and had left no room for other boarders.

King Fortune was sitting on the top storey of his palace looking silently out over the city. His generals tried to distract him with plans for military campaigns and his courtesans tried to distract him with charming words, but he paid no attention to any of them. Suddenly he said, "There is a fire burning just outside the southern gate. There is someone walking around it. Who is this? How has this happened? Where are my guards? This must be someone from the royal family of Kosala, someone who will stop at nothing to kill me in revenge!" And from that day on he slept badly, dreaming that someone was trying to kill him.

But Fair slipped out of the city as soon as the gates opened at dawn, and went to live in the forest. First he stayed in a hut and kept a sacred fire burning for his parents, yet he was not able to cry and felt nothing but hatred. Then he recited hymns. Then he went naked and covered his body in ashes from a cremation ground, drinking water from a human skull. Then he ate nothing but fallen fruits and sat with his body exposed to the noonday sun, surrounded by twelve fires. But still he shed no tears, and his chest felt as cold as the ice that envelops the world at the end of the aeon.

One day Fair thought, "It is no use. My heart is full of the poison of hatred. Prayers cannot drive out this poison. Fasting and pain cannot drive it out. I will be free only when I have killed the King of Benares." So he washed the ash and dirt from his body, put on his clothes, slung his lute over his shoulder and left the forest. He joined a group of traders headed for Benares. Before many days he was inside the city, and he headed straight for the royal palace. At the elephant stables he stopped and asked to see the master of the elephants.

"Yes, young man, you wish to speak to me?"

"Master, I wish to learn your art. I wish to know what elephants eat, what they fear and desire, how they may be trained and befriended. I am prepared to study the four sutras and the thirteen sastras on the art of elephant-knowledge. To be apprentice to you is my only desire."

"Very well, young man, I accept you."

So Fair lived in the elephant stables, sleeping in the straw beside the elephants. He was given enough food to keep the spirit in the body, and he did his job well, but his sole purpose was to get close to the king.

One evening he took out his lute and sat just outside the stable door. He began to play and sing. He sang such a sad song that the elephants wept, the mice wept, and the crows outside on the trees wept. As the wind carried the song to the palace, everyone in the palace wept. Only Fair's eyes were dry.

The King was sitting outside on the top storey of his palace taking the air, surrounded by his attendants, flunkies and hangers-on. Soon they were all crying their eyes out. Fortune said:

"Find out who is singing and playing the lute." When those he had sent returned they reported, "It is some young man or other, Your Imperial Majesty, who works in the elephant stables."

"Bring him here." So they brought Fair, and Fortune said, "Are you the young man who has been making this music?"

"I am, Your Majesty."

"Then sing and play for us."

Fair did so, and soon the whole company was wringing the tears out of their robes.

"You must not be human, young man," said Fortune. "For you sing and play as if the world's heart were breaking, yet you do not shed even one tear. Are you a Gandhabba, a water-sprite, a ghost?"

"I am a human being, Your Majesty. But I cannot weep, for some poison has entered my heart."

"Then come and stay with us," said Fortune, "and wait on us and play for us, and perhaps some way will be found to expel this poison."

"Very well, Your Majesty," said Fair.

So Fair became the personal attendant, confidante and musician of Fortune. And Fortune grew to love him.

One day Fortune said, "Prepare the chariot, my dear young man, and let us go hunting. Perhaps hunting will drive the poison from your heart."

So Fair prepared the chariot and drove the King deep into the forest, away from the city walls, away from the army outposts. As the day wore on the King grew very tired, so he said, "Unharness the horses, my dear. I am exhausted and must rest."

When Fair had unharnessed the horses Fortune lay down on the earth—his robe stretched under him, his head on Fair's lap—and fell fast asleep. And Fair thought, "Now is the time. My preparations have borne fruit; my revenge is at hand." And with his right hand he drew his sword from the scabbard to cut the king's head from his body. But Fortune came awake with a start, saying:

"Oh, who will save me from this dream! Whenever I fall asleep I am pursued by the son of the King of Kosala!"

Fair rose and, with his left hand, grasped the King by the hair.

"This is no dream. I am Fair, the son of the King of Kosala. The time has come to avenge my parents and to appease my hatred. You, Fortune, invaded Kosala. You stole, you killed, you drove my parents into exile. When you found them you took them and had their heads shaved with a razor and paraded them through the streets to the terrible sound of the Panava drum. Every day I hear that sound and every day I see that sight! How tightly they were bound! How it must have hurt them!"

And a tear ran down Fair's cheek.

"Just before my parents reached the southern gate my father saw me in the crowd, and he cried out:

> 'Dear One, beware
> the poison of hatred.
> Hatred ends not by hatred.
> Dear One, beware.
> For hatred ends
> Only by letting it go.' "

When he had repeated his father's words, a second tear rolled down Fair's cheek, then a third. And he began to weep. He wept as if the world's heart was breaking, and as he did so the poison left his body. Trembling, he took his sword and placed it on the ground before Fortune, saying:

"Now at last I have laid it down. Kill me if you wish."

But Fortune embraced him and said, "My dear young man, you have given me my life. Now let me give you yours."

So Fair, son of the King of Kosala, and Fortune, King of Benares, gave each other their lives. And they took a solemn vow never to hurt or deceive each other. They were received in the city with shouts, applause and the trumpeting of many elephants.

Some tellers of this tale go on to tell of thrones restored and daughters given in marriage, but I have told you all you need to know. And since all things must end, even stories, I shall end here.

Sons and daughters of good family, I have told you the tale of King Fate. There is no one in the three-fold universe more addicted than kings to hatred and the sword, so let us join our palms in gratitude for the king who taught his son, and thereby this age, how to lay them down at last.

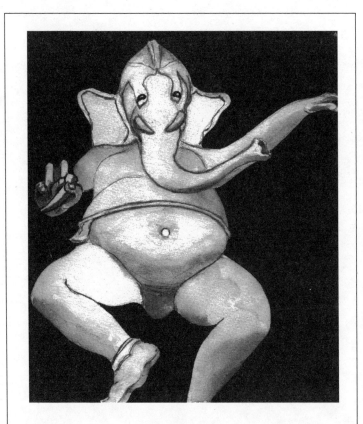

TELL IT TO THE WALLS

RETOLD BY DIANE SCHOEMPERLEN

AFTER HER HUSBAND DIED suddenly of a heart attack at the age of fifty-nine, Mabel Patterson's whole life changed. Although they had lived a happy and comfortable life together on the farm for over thirty years, Victor Patterson's unexpected passing left his wife in dire straits. He was a good but forgetful man who had made many bad investments and often neglected to pay the bills. He had always meant to buy life insurance but, sadly, he never got around to it. Victor, like most mortals, thought he had all the time in the world. After his death, Mabel found herself so poor that she had to move in with her two sons and their wives.

Neither of her sons, Charlie or Steve, had ever shown any inclination to become farmers. Some years before their father's death they had moved to the city a hundred miles away. After both had found good jobs and got married, they pooled their resources and bought a big duplex in the city. They all lived there together, Charlie and his wife Rose on the main floor, Steve and his wife Kathy upstairs. Both Rose and Kathy were now expecting their first children. They said Mabel could live in the basement. They said she would have her own bedroom down there, her own bathroom, and her very own TV. They said she would make lots of new friends in the city. And, they said, after the babies were born in the spring, Mabel would be able to see her grandchildren every day. Wouldn't it be wonderful? She would never be lonely again.

At first it *was* wonderful. But soon everything began to change. One day both Rose and Kathy were not feeling well. Rose asked Mabel if she wouldn't mind just washing the kitchen floor and putting in a few loads of laundry. Kathy upstairs wondered if Mabel wouldn't mind just vacuuming the stairs and cleaning the oven. She had some ironing that needed doing too. Mabel was happy to help.

When Charlie came home from work that night, he was very hungry and tired. Rose was still resting so Mabel made her older son a big supper. Charlie complained that the salad was wilted and the meat was not spicy enough but he ate it anyway. He also said the kitchen floor was still dirty even though Mabel had washed it that very morning. When Mabel took a tray to Rose in the bedroom, Rose said she couldn't eat because she was so upset by the fact that Mabel had shrunk her favourite sweater in the wash. After supper Charlie asked Mabel to do the dishes because he was too tired.

When Steve upstairs came home late from work, he complained loudly because there was no supper waiting for him. Kathy was still resting so Mabel went upstairs and made her younger son a big supper. Steve complained that the rice was sticky and the meat was too spicy but he ate it anyway. He also said the stairs were still dirty even though Mabel had vacuumed them that very afternoon. When Mabel took a tray to Kathy in the bedroom, Kathy said she couldn't eat because she was so upset by the fact that Mabel had scorched her favourite blouse with the iron. After supper Mabel did the dishes because Steve wanted to watch TV.

The next day both Rose and Kathy were feeling a bit better. They were well enough to lie on their living-room couches all day watching soap operas and phoning their friends. So Mabel spent all morning running up and down between the two households doing all the chores. Then she spent all afternoon running back and forth to the grocery store to satisfy the cravings of the two pregnant women. Rose wanted sweet pickles. Kathy wanted butterscotch ripple ice cream. Then Rose wanted orange sherbet. Then Kathy wanted a pineapple upside-down cake. This went on all afternoon until finally Mabel had been to the grocery store twelve times.

Although Rose and Kathy were well enough to eat, they were not well enough to cook. So once again Mabel prepared a big supper both upstairs and down. Once again her sons and their wives complained bitterly while stuffing themselves. They criticized her cooking and everything else she had done for them that day. After supper, Mabel once again did the dishes for both households because they all said they had better things to do.

By the time Mabel got back to her room in the basement, she was too tired and unhappy to watch her very own TV. It didn't work right half the time anyway. So she lay down on her bed and cried herself to sleep.

The next day was the same. And the next and the next and the next. Mabel did everything for her sons and their wives and then listened to them complain that everything she had done was wrong. They took turns telling her how stupid she was. Then she would go down to her basement room and cry.

It went on and on the same. Mabel could not understand how her sons who had once been happy, loving children on the farm had turned into such mean and nasty men in the city. She did not understand why they had both married such mean and lazy women. Mabel had no one to tell her troubles to. She'd had no time to make new friends in the city. She didn't want to make trouble in the households. After all, her sons and their wives had taken her in when she had nowhere else to go. Besides, she was afraid that if she complained about how they treated her, they would throw her out onto the street.

So day after day Mabel swallowed her hurt and her anger. She kept it all inside and gradually her body began to swell. The more she swallowed, the fatter she got. Soon she was so fat that she could barely get up and down the stairs between the two households. She could no longer fit into the bathtub in her very own bathroom. She could no longer roll over in the little bed in her very own bedroom. She was so fat that sometimes she could hardly even breathe.

Now when her sons and their wives had finished criticizing her for her bad cooking, her inept housekeeping and her general stupidity, they would go on to ridicule her ever-increasing size. They said she was always eating like a pig. Apparently they hadn't noticed that she was so busy looking after them that she never had time to eat much herself. They said she was as big as a cow, a moose, an elephant, as big as the Goodyear blimp. They shuddered, they said, to think what their dear departed father would say if he could see her now. Steve said Victor must be rolling over in his grave.

One Saturday afternoon, Charlie and Rose and Steve and Kathy decided to go to a concert in the park. Mabel, who seldom got to go anywhere except the grocery store, said she would like to go too. But Charlie said they were too ashamed to be seen with her in public. People would point and stare, Rose said. Little children would think she was a monster made of blubber, Kathy said. They would run away screaming with fright. Besides, Steve said, she was too fat to fit in the car. Charlie said they'd have to tie her to the roof rack to get her to the park. The four of them set off for the concert laughing.

Mabel, left behind, could not bear to spend the afternoon alone in her basement room. She grabbed her purse and her coat (even though it didn't fit her any more) and walked to the bus stop at the corner of the street. She got on the first bus that came along. She was so fat that the driver charged her double because she took up two seats all by herself. The bus took her to the northern edge of the city.

She got off and she walked. Because of her massive size, she could not move very fast. Puffing and sweating, she kept stopping to catch her breath. Gradually she left the city behind. The road curled through countryside that reminded her of the farm she had shared with Victor for so long. This made her feel even sadder and lonelier than usual.

Just as Mabel thought she might collapse from the effort of walking so far, she spotted a deserted farmhouse just off the road to the left. She laboured up the laneway towards the old brick building. The windows were all broken and the roof was gone. She went inside.

Standing in the middle of the broken-down house, Mabel was finally overwhelmed by misery and despair. She couldn't keep her troubles inside for a minute longer. She had to talk to someone even though there was no one there.

So Mabel told the wall in front of her all about her older son, Charlie. Charlie who said she was as big as a cow, Charlie who complained because the floor was dirty and the supper was not spicy enough, Charlie who said they'd have to tie her to the roof rack, Charlie who was ashamed to be seen with her in public. When she was finished, the first wall gave way beneath the weight of her woes. The bricks crashed down in a heap and lay on the ground in a cloud of dust. Mabel's body grew a little lighter.

Then she turned to the second wall and told it all about her daughter-in-law Rose. Rose who said she was as big as a moose, Rose who yelled at her for shrinking her favourite clothes in the wash, Rose who said people would point and stare, Rose who told her everyday that she was fat and stupid. Down came the second wall into another dusty heap of bricks. Mabel's body grew lighter still.

To the third wall she told the tales of her younger son, Steve. Steve who said she was as big as an elephant, Steve who complained because the stairs were dirty and the supper was too spicy, Steve who said she was too fat to fit in the car, Steve who said Victor would die of shame to see her now if he weren't already dead. The third wall collapsed too.

Then, feeling even lighter, Mabel turned to the remaining wall and told it all about her daughter-in-law Kathy. Kathy who said she was as big as the Goodyear blimp, Kathy who swore at her for scorching her favourite blouse with an iron, Kathy who said little children would run away screaming at the sight of her, Kathy who said she was probably the fattest, stupidest woman in the world. The fourth wall went tumbling to the ground.

Standing in the ruins of the old farmhouse with rubble and dust all around her, Mabel felt better than she had since Victor died. She looked down at herself and was surprised to discover that her body had shrunk back to its original size. All the hurt and anger she had swallowed had finally been released and all her fat had disappeared.

Mabel put on her coat and began the long journey home. When she got to the edge of the city, she once again took the first bus that came along. It was the same driver but he didn't recognize her. He told her she was looking lovely and he let her ride for free. She got off the bus downtown and went into a huge department store. She went upstairs to the cafeteria and had a cup of tea. She struck up a conversation with the lonely-looking overweight woman at the next table. They parted with a promise to meet again next Saturday, same place, same time, for another cup of tea.

Then Mabel went down to the third floor and bought two dozen balls of wool and some knitting needles. In the electronics department on the second floor she bought a cassette player with little headphones and a whole box of tapes. Back on the busy street Mabel found the right bus and went home.

When her sons and their wives arrived home from the concert an hour later, all four of them started right away yelling because the house was a mess and there was nothing to eat. They thundered down the basement stairs and threw open the door of Mabel's very own bedroom. Their faces were red and their four mean mouths fell open at the sight of Mabel with her headphones on, humming and smiling and knitting bonnets and booties for the babies who would be born soon. She looked up at them and grinned. Then, with one thin arm, she waved them away.

GLOSSARY

Adam's Peak   *Sri Pada* in Sinhalese and *Sivanolipadam* in Tamil. Between December Full Moon Day and May Full Moon Day many people go on pilgrimages to this mountain top.

Anuradhapura   *Anuradhapuram* in Tamil. An ancient capital and a sacred city. In this city is the sacred bo-tree, the oldest tree in the world. Originally the bo-tree was a sapling taken from the Bodhi tree (the tree under which the Buddha attained enlightenment) in Bodh Gaya, India.

ambalama   Resting place for travellers, especially after dark.

bandicoot   Large rat found in India and Sri Lanka.

Benares   A city in north-east India in the state of Uttar Pradesh, on the Ganges River. Also known as Varanasi or Kasi. For Hindus, the holiest city in India. Benares was well known in ancient times and the Buddha preached his first sermon in its vicinity. The city is officially known today as Varanasi, but we have chosen to use the form familiar to most Western readers.

bodhisatta   A word in the Pali language, the sacred language of Sri Lankan Buddhism. The term refers to the being who in a later incarnation or rebirth would become the Buddha.

bodhisattva   Sanskrit term meaning the same as Pali *bodhisatta*.

Brahma   Brahma, creator of the universe, is part of a holy trinity in Hinduism including Shiva and Vishnu. Brahma plays a role in Buddhism also.

Buddha   The Enlightened One. The teacher who lived in North India in the sixth and fifth centuries B.C., and from whom Buddhism takes its name.

Chola (King)   A powerful south Indian Tamil dynasty that at one time extended an empire over parts of South Asia.

Companions	Also called the Companions of the Prophet. Followers of the Prophet Muhammad who had direct, personal contact with him.
congee	Sinhalese word for porridge.
devale	Sacred place where devotees offer food and other gifts to win favours. Most of the gods and devils addressed in devales are original Hindu deities.
Gamarala	Sinhalese word for village headman (leader).
Ganesha	Hindu god—the elephant-headed god of wisdom. Son of Parvati and Shiva. He is also the god of auspiciousness and success, known as the remover of obstacles and as the one who subdues detrimental forces.
Garuda	The divine bird, half man, half eagle, who in Hindu legend was the arch-enemy of snakes. Vishnu sometimes rode upon Garuda's wings. In Buddhist stories, garudas were noted for, among other things, their incessant warfare with the *nagas*, a mythical race of serpents.
Hanuman	The monkey-god who assisted Rama, his mother was a monkey named Anjana and his father was Vayu, the wind god. Hanuman is the only figure to appear in both Hindu epics the *Ramayana* and the *Mahabharata*.
Indra	An Indian *deva*, or god, known from the earliest Indian scriptures and revered in ancient times as the warrior king of the gods. In Buddhist literature and in Puranic Hinduism he is often portrayed as well-meaning but somewhat simple-minded, his place as supreme deity having been taken over by other divine personalities.
jak tree	A tree that produces large egg-shaped fruits. Each fruit is very heavy. Jak fruit is boiled and served with scraped coconut. The wood of this tree is strong, used to make very durable furniture.
kaludodol	Sweetmeat prepared with coconut milk, rice flour and treacle.
Karunavai	A kind of prayer, and positive greeting, that can be spoken by people as they descend Adam's Peak. They will say this word to those who are climbing past them or walking to the mountain. A Sinhalese word, Karunavai means *be compassionate* or *have compassion*.
Kasi	Ancient Indian kingdom, the capital city of which was Benares.

Kathirakaman	*Kataragama*. A sacred town in the island's south-east where the god Skanda's temple (devala) is situated.
kitul tree	Same as *palmyra* tree.
Kosala	Ancient Indian kingdom that rose during the Buddha's lifetime to a position of great power in northern India, annexing the kingdom of Kasi.
Krishna	Krishna is an avatar. He is a reincarnation of Lord Vishnu, one of the Hindu trinity. Lord Vishnu is known as the preserver of the universe. Krishna is also known as the "blue god."
kumbuk	A large tree. Usually grows near streams but it is often planted near wells because of the belief in its cooling properties. A pulp can be made out of the kumbuk's leaves and applied to one's head for a cooling effect.
Kuveni	According to Sinhalese legends, Kuveni married Prince Vijaya. She represents the aborigines or the first settlers of Sri Lanka.
Mahabharata	A Hindu epic, and one of the longest connected narratives in world literature. The *Mahabharata* deals with the conflict between two related families, the Pandavas and the Kauravas.
mahout	Hindi word for elephant-driver, keeper. In Tamil the name is *yanai pahan*. In Sinhalese, *atgovva*.
Maya	Magic power, appearance, illusion. The way the gods manifest or display the world as opposed to the essence of the world as perceived by seers and saints.
Medina	Located in western Saudi Arabia, Medina is, with Mecca, one of the two most honoured cities in Islam. The Muslim calendar dates from the arrival of the Prophet Muhammad in Medina on September 20, A.D. 622.
Pali	An Indo-European language closely related to Sanskrit. Pali is the sacred language of Theravada Buddhism, the form of Buddhism most common in Sri Lanka.
palmyra	Tall palm tree producing useful wood, fibre, leaves for thatching and weaving, and sap for sugar and liquor.
panava	Pali word for cymbal or small drum with jarring sound.
Pote gura	A Sinhalese word for narrator.
The Prophet	Muhammad. Muslims recognize the existence of a series of prophets or messengers of God, but Muhammad is acknowledged as the last of the prophets.

rakkhasa	(*Rakshasa* in Sinhalese.) Pali term for malevolent, semi-divine being or demon.
rakkhasi	(*Rakshasini* in Sinhalese.) Female form of the above.
Ramayana	The story of Rama and Sita, and of Rama's war with Ravana, the King of Lanka. The *Ramayana* is one of the two great Hindu epics, the other being The *Mahabharata*.
sambol	A mixture of scraped coconut, hot red chillies, salt, lime juice and onions. It is eaten in small amounts with rice or bread.
sastra	Treatise. A religious or scientific work.
Sathipattana	In Pali, *Satipatthana*. The *Satipatthana Sutta* is a famous Buddhist scripture about the establishing of correct mindfulness or awareness.
Savatthi	A Pali word. In the Buddha's time, Savatthi was the capital city of Kosala. The Buddha often taught in Savatthi.
Shiva	One of the Hindu trinity, with Brahma and Vishnu. He is the god of destruction, at once destroyer and revivifier.
sutra	A rule, manual or sacred text.
thovila	A therapeutic religious event that occurs in the "little tradition" in Sinhalese Buddhism. When people are sick, or there is a natural disaster, people get together and perform a thovila in order to propitiate evil gods and demons.
three-fold universe	In Buddhism, usually refers to the three realms of the universe: the realms of sensuality, materiality and immateriality. Different beings inhabit each realm.
toddy	The word derives from the Hindi word *tari*. Fresh or fermented sap of various palm trees—for example, the palmyra.
Vijaya	Prince Vijaya is known, in the *Mahavamsa*, as the founding father of the Sinhala nation. Born in west Bengal, Vijaya came to Sri Lanka during the fifth century B.C. and became the first king.
Vissakamma	Indian deva or god: the "all maker," the gods' architect, maker, artist.

NOTES ON THE RETELLINGS

The Monkey King. Retold from H.T. Francis's translation of the Mahakapi-Jataka, in *The Jataka, or Stories of the Buddha's Former Births*, Vol. 3 (Cambridge University Press, 1895).

How the Landlord Went to Heaven. Previously published in George Keyt's *Folk Stories of Sri Lanka* (Colombo: Lake House, 1974)—a collection of tales told to Keyt in Sinhala by people in villages and in rural schools.

Brighter Still. Retold from his translation of the Pali Jataka legend Nigrodhamiga-Jataka (Graeme MacQueen, 1994).

Lord Krishna and Kaliya. A retelling of the Hindu legend.

The Resting Hill. Retold from P. Kandasamy's oral telling of a Tamil tale.

The Chola King. Retold from P. Poologasingham's version of the Tamil folktale.

The Deer, the Tortoise and the Kaerala Bird. A retelling of the Kurunga-Miga Jataka. A version of this story can be found in *The Jataka, or Stories of the Buddha's Former Births*, Vol. 1 (Cambridge University Press, 1895).

Water Under a Rock. Retold from Robert Chalmers' translation of the Vannupatha-Jataka, in *The Jataka, or Stories of the Buddha's Former Births*, Vol. 1 (Cambridge University Press, 1895).

Two Friends by the Villu. A retelling of a Sri Lankan folktale.

The Vulture. Retold from W.H.D. Rouse's translation of the Gijjha-Jataka, in *The Jataka, or Stories of the Buddha's Former Births*, Vol. 2 (Cambridge University Press, 1895).

The Hopper. A retelling of a Tamil folktale.

The Dog Who Drank from Socks. Retold from Jezima Ismail's telling of a Muslim tale.

Narada's Lesson. Retold from a translation/telling of the Hindu legend by Heinrich Zimmer in *Myths and Symbols in Indian Art and Civilization* (Princeton University Press, 1946).

Power Misused. A retelling of a Sinhalese folktale.

The Unicorn and the Grapevine. An original story inspired by the Ruru-Jataka which can be found in *The Jataka, or Stories of the Buddha's Former Births*, Vol. 4 (Cambridge University Press, 1895). The quotation that appears at the beginning of the story is from "The Antelope" found in *Once the Buddha Was a Monkey*, a translation of Arya Sura's Jatakamala by Peter Khoroche (University of Chicago Press, 1989.)

Scarless Face. Retold from Robert Chalmers' translation of the Mahilamukha-Jataka, in *The Jataka, or Stories of the Buddha's Former Births*, Vol. 1 (Cambridge University Press, 1895).

The Cycle of Revenge. An original story/retelling inspired by a story from the *Saddharmaratnavaliya* entitled "The Demoness Kali," translated from the Sinhalese by Ranjini Obeyesekere (State University of New York Press, 1991). Used as a reference, with permission of the translator.

The Monkey and the Crocodile. A retelling of a popular South Asian tale, widely known and appearing in different forms, including a Jataka tale version.

Garuda and the Snake. Retold from W.H.D. Rouse's translation of the Uraga-Jataka, in *The Jataka, or Stories of the Buddha's Former Births*, Vol. 2 (Cambridge University Press, 1895).

Just Like the Rest. Retold from his translation of the Pali Jataka legend Sarabha-Miga-Jataka (Graeme MacQueen, 1994). A version can also be found in *The Jataka, or Stories of the Buddha's Former Births*, Vol. 4 (Cambridge University Press, 1895).

The Rupee. Retelling of a Tamil tale.

Is the River Asleep? Retold from K. Sivathamby's telling of a Tamil folktale.

Hanuman and Sita. A retelling of the story from the Hindu epic the *Ramayana*.

Angulimala. Retold from translations by Graeme MacQueen (1994) and I.B. Horner (*The Collection of the Middle Length Sayings*, Pali Text Society: 1957), of the Pali story *The Angulimala Sutta*.

Two Stories of Andare the Court Jester. Previously published in George Keyt's *Folk Stories of Sri Lanka*.

The Road to Butterfly Mountain. A retelling of a Sinhalese tale, previously published in Manel Ratnatunga's collection of Sinhalese, Tamil and Muslim tales, *Folktales of Sri Lanka* (New Delhi: Sterling Publishers, 1979).

A Changed Snake. A retelling of a folktale popular in both Sri Lanka and India.

Akbar and Birbal. A retelling of a popular Muslim tale. Inspired by Monisha Mukundan's retelling in *Akbar and Birbal, Tales of Humour* (New Delhi: Rupa & Co., 1992) by Monisha Mukundan.

Mouthful of Pearls. A retelling inspired by the story of Subha the Nun (from the *Therigatha*), translated from the Pali by Susan Murcotte in her book entitled *The First Buddhist Women—Translations and Commentary on the Therigatha* (Berkeley: Parallax Press, 1991). Used as a reference, with permission of the translator.

The Camel Who Cried in the Sun. A retelling of a Muslim tale.

How the Gods and Demons Learned to Play Together A modern version of the myth of the origin of drama from the third-century work the *Natyasastra*.

The Great Journey. Retold from a version by J.M. MacFie of the legend from the *Mahabharata*, in his book *Myths and Legends of India* (New York: Scribner & Sons, 1924).

Fate and Fortune. Retold from his translation of the story of *Dighavu* found in the *Mahavagga*, a book from the Buddhist monastic discipline. A version of this story can also be found in *The Grateful Elephant and Other Stories Translated from the Pali*, by E.W. Burlingame (New Haven: Yale University Press, 1923).

Tell It to the Walls. Retold from A.K. Ramanujan's retelling of a Tamil folktale, which appeared in his book *Folktales from India, A Selection of Oral Tales from Twenty-Two Languages* (New York: Pantheon Books, 1991).

ON WORLD LITERACY OF CANADA

World Literacy of Canada (WLC) is a non-profit organization that works to raise awareness in Canada about Canadian and international literacy issues and fund literacy projects in developing countries. Founded forty years ago, WLC was the first non-governmental organization in Canada devoted to supporting literacy and non-formal education projects overseas. In 1955 a small group of Canadians concerned with supporting literacy initiatives in India began the work of WLC through education and community development programs. WLC continues to focus its efforts in South Asia, primarily India.

WLC's concept of literacy goes beyond one of reading, writing and numeracy to one of ensuring people acquire the life skills and knowledge necessary for development. We believe that literacy is rooted in the prevailing social, cultural and economic conditions of a country. It is linked to poverty, disadvantage and exclusion. Literacy is an essential element in the struggle for justice, human dignity and equality, and it is indeed an indispensable building block of social and economic change.

WLC believes that in order for economic change to improve lives, people need to be involved in the development process—defining their needs and planning, organizing and executing programs to meet those needs. Literacy is a basic skill that enables people to participate in this process. Reading and writing are tools that empower people. People who cannot read or write are unable to function fully within their society. With improved listening, speaking, reading, writing and numeracy skills, people gain self-confidence and a greater degree of control over their lives.

WLC recognizes that literacy is linked to all development. Policies aimed at alleviating poverty, reducing infant mortality and improving public health, protecting the environment, strengthening human rights, improving international understanding and enriching culture, as much as those aiming to gain competitiveness in advanced technology, are essentially incomplete if they do not incorporate an appropriate literacy and educational strategy.

In working towards a just and democratic world, WLC's vision has evolved since 1955 to identifying three main roles for the organization: (1) to design and implement community-based literacy and development programs; (2) to establish and enhance relationships with Southern partners that strengthen those partners and their capacity to respond effectively to community needs and priorities; and (3) to promote public awareness of interdependence and engagement in global problems and global solutions.

With the launch of The Monkey King & Other Stories, WLC celebrates 40 years of commitment by scores of dedicated volunteers and low-paid staff who have shared the belief in the potential of individuals. World Literacy of Canada gratefully acknowledges the support and contributions of the following people and organizations whose generosity and dedication have made this book possible: Sri Lanka Canada Development Fund, HarperCollins Publishers Canada, all the contributing writers, David Bolduc, Chitra Ranawake and Graeme MacQueen. Special thanks to the editor, Griffin Ondaatje, who has put together a great book with lots of fun stories.

All proceeds from the sale of the book will be matched by the Canadian International Development Agency (CIDA) and used to support literacy programs. For further information on how you can help, please contact: World Literacy of Canada, 59 Front Street East, 2nd Floor, Toronto, Ontario, M5E 1B3. Telephone: (416) 863-6262, Fax: (416) 601-6984.